MURDER
ON
THE
BOULEVARD

BY

KORI DONAHUE

This is a work of fiction. Names, characters, places, and incidents either are the product of the author's imagination or are used fictitiously, and any resemblance to actual persons, living or dead, businesses, companies, events, or locales is entirely coincidental.

Kori Donahue
Visit my website at www.blondeepisodes.com
Fiction. Historical Fiction. Mystery.

Printed in the United States of America
ISBN: 978-0615484655

First Printing: April 2011

For my parents, who have given me everything they have, and would do anything for me. Without your constant love and support, I would not be as blessed as I truly am today. I owe you everything.

For my brother, who encouraged and pushed me every step of the way. Without you, I would never have finished this task and I love you every day for it.

For my students, thank you to all my current and former students for allowing me to share my love of reading and writing with you. You keep me young, make me laugh, and allow me to do a job I love more and more everyday.

Lastly, for Nicolette Fischer. Thank you for suggesting I join NaNoWriMo. Without your idea, I would still be saying, "I want to..."

Chapter 1

Bobbi did whatever it took to make sure everyone liked her, or at least think they liked her. Her confident, stiletto-clad strut convinced the world, "I can do anything better than you."

But that confidence attracted trouble. As an independent woman living in a conservative man's world, she felt an overwhelming need to break free.

At 28, her family chastised her for being single. They often called her an "old maid," telling her that if she weren't so selfish she would have a husband by now.

It wasn't that she didn't want to be married; it was just that she refused to settle for some man who expected her to be his slave. After watching her mother completely lose herself over the years, she couldn't understand why anyone would want to become nothing more than a caretaker. Her father had expected her mother to wait on him hand and foot. She rarely, if ever, was *allowed* to visit with friends or take a day off alone. Bobbi promised herself that she would make more of her own life.

Bobbi's girlfriends were a little threatened by her. Truth be told, they didn't want their darling, single friend around their husbands. Men get bored, and with someone like Bobbi around, it would be easy for them to become a little too "fresh." Because of this, friends were constantly trying to set her up. The men Bobbi were introduced to were boring, too traditional, and often insecure. They failed to realize that times were changing and the world no longer revolved around them and what was in their pants.

Bobbi wasn't wild by any means, but enjoyed a stiff drink (vodka tonic), her cigarettes, and the occasional company of men. She didn't sleep around, and only became involved romantically with men she considered serious, or a "boyfriend."

Working at Fitzgerald, Patrick, and Smith was not particularly fun. Bobbi was a secretary for James P. Fitzgerald, one of the law firm's partners. Since it was 1955, Bobbi understood that there were no female attorneys in the firm. Women were secretaries, not lawyers. Maybe it wouldn't be so bad if Bobbi didn't feel like a piece of meat at the office.

Rather than noticing how hard she worked, her boss made her uncomfortable with comments like, "Hey beautiful…could you bring your sweet behind in here with my coffee?" or, "Baby, your ass looks great in that suit." Just once she'd like to toss that coffee right in his lap. A man's world—yuck.

Bobbi's blood started to boil at the thoughts of Fitzgerald's outrageous comments when she looked up to see a handsome stranger standing at the elevator. *Who is that?* She wondered. It couldn't be someone new at the firm. These stiffs have been here since the beginning of time. *Wow, he almost looks like…*she lost her train of thought as the refined man walked toward her. Unfortunately his looks caught her so off guard she lost her voice as well. Mute, she stared at him until he finally broke the silence.

"Excuse me, but do you happen to know where James Fitzgerald's office is?"

"Yes, follow me, I'm his secretary."

"Oh, great, I'm sorry I didn't catch your name?" He said.

"Miss Brooks, Bobbi Brooks."

"It's nice to meet you Miss Bobbi Brooks. My name is Howard Starks."

"I will let Mr. Fitzgerald know you're here. He's expecting you, I assume?" She asked.

"Oh, let's hope so." He said with a grin.

Strange, I don't remember seeing anything on Mr. Fitzgerald's calendar about meeting with a Mr. Starks,

Bobbi thought to herself. *Oh well, the old coot probably scheduled something without telling me.*

"Mr. Fitzgerald, there is a Mr. Starks here to see you, sir."

"What? Are you sure? Tell him I stepped out for a smoke," Fitzgerald replied.

"Ok, whatever you say, sir. I will let him know and reschedule."

"No! Don't reschedule, just tell him I'm out." Fitzgerald yelled at her. "Yes, sir." Fitzgerald certainly seemed out of sorts today.

On the way back to the lobby, Bobbi thought about the intriguing Mr. Starks. He gave the impression of total self-confidence with a touch of smugness, as if he knew something no one else did. What was he hiding? His good looks were charming but there was something dangerous, and deliciously appealing, about the stranger.

"Mr. Starks? She called out to him. Mr. Fitzgerald has stepped out and has asked me to reschedule your appointment."

"Oh, he did, did he?" Mr. Starks replied. That sounds about right. Just tell James that I will be back tomorrow around the same time, and I expect him to be here waiting for me."

With that, he smirked, turned, and walked off toward the elevator.

Strange, Bobbi thought. What was all that all about?

Chapter 2

The next day, Bobbi returned to work preoccupied. She hated to admit it, but she was actually excited to see Howard Starks, and had dressed to impress. She had tried to focus on other things the night before, but couldn't seem to get his smile out of her mind. There was definitely something sinister about him, and for some reason, she was attracted to it.

Around the same time she had seen him the previous afternoon, Mr. Starks came walking through the lobby. "Good afternoon, Mr. Starks. I told Mr. Fitzgerald you would be coming in today, but I can't seem to locate him." She said. "I think he might have taken ill, and returned home for the afternoon. I'm so sorry. I wish there was something I could do."

"You can, Miss Brooks. Have lunch with me today?" Starks asked her.

Bobbi wanted so desperately to spend time with this man that it took everything in her not to scream "Yes!" "Well, I am about to take lunch," she said, "So I guess I can head out with you."

"Great. Where would you like to go?" Starks led her out of the building.

Bobbi couldn't believe she was walking down the boulevard with this dashing, secretive man. *I have to find out more about him, even though it feels like he might be hiding something,* she thought.

Howard Starks was charming, funny, and of course sexy. Bobbi couldn't remember being so nervous and turned on by a man at the same time. She laughed at everything he said, and could only think of the next time she would see him. He seemed to be enamored of her as well. He asked her all about her family, why she wasn't married yet (of course), and how she liked her job at the firm.

He seemed to be more interested in what Bobbi had to say than any man she had ever met. After lunch, he asked for her phone number and if he could take her out to dinner Friday night. She said yes, of course and floated back to work to finish out the day. She couldn't wait to spend a night out with Howard Starks.

Friday night came after what felt like the longest week ever. Bobbi made sure to wear her nicest lingerie, (just in case), a new chocolate brown dress, matching pumps, an adorable hat, and perfect gloves. The only thing she was missing was the matching handbag, which she had borrowed from her friend Sue. After spraying on the last of her Chanel No. 5, she sat down impatiently. Why did she get ready so early? She wondered. Now, she would just sit and fidget waiting for Howard.

Speak of the devil, she thought, as the doorbell rang. *Early*, she thought, *I like that. It shows he's anxious to see me.* Bobbi answered the door and they were on their way.

"Where are we going this evening, Howard?"

"I thought we would try the new restaurant around the corner, Deco Lounge, if that's ok with you."

"Of course, that sounds perfect," Bobbi responded. I've been dying to go there."

After using his influence to get a great table, Howard escorted Bobbi to her seat. A wonderful singer was performing, and the atmosphere of the lounge was absolutely perfect. Bobbi couldn't have asked for a better date. Howard was good-looking, funny, easy to talk to, and sexy as hell. Bobbi decided to have a few cocktails and let her hair down a little.

After two vodka tonics, she was feeling pretty good. All she could think of was kissing Howard and whispering sweet nothings in his ear. They decided to leave the lounge and head back to her place for a nightcap.

Bobbi turned on some music by her favorite singer, Peggy Lee, and before she knew it, they were in bed together. Everything was perfect. Bobbi couldn't remember being with a man who was so caring and concerned about her. He wasn't selfish at all. After they both lay spent, smoking, and dreamy-eyed, Howard rolled over and looked at her.

"You're incredible, Bobbi," He told her. I haven't met a girl like you before. There's something about you honey and I can't wait to find out more about you."

Bobbi wanted so badly to tell him she felt the same way, but she didn't want to share too much, yet. Howard made her so nervous.

"When can we see each other again?" She asked.

"Tomorrow, baby. I want to see as much of you as possible, if you know what I mean." He said. *Oh my*, Bobbi thought.

Chapter 3

Saturday and Sunday came and went, and Bobbi was finally back to work on Monday. Howard had spent the entire weekend with Bobbi, but now it was time to return to the real world. After the fun weekend she has, Bobbi was not anxious to return to the firm at all.

On her way in, Mr. Fitzgerald almost ran her over. "I'm sorry Bobbi, I'm in a huge hurry...I'll explain later."

Peculiar. He had been acting strange since last week. What was going on? She wondered. Oh well, maybe he was having issues with his horrible wife.

Bobbi barely got anything done. All she could think about was Howard. The way he touched her, looked at her, kissed her, and made her feel about herself consumed her thoughts. She couldn't wait to see him again tomorrow. He had work to do tonight, so they would have to miss each other a little, which might not be such a bad thing, she thought.

Bobbi had finally just dozed off when the phone rang. "Hello?" She answered groggily.

"Bobbi! It's Howard! I need you to meet me at Joe's Coffee Shop on 2nd right away! Can you come now?"

"Howard? She answered him, confused. What's wrong? Are you okay? What time is it?"

"I just need you to come right away," he replied. "Can you meet me?"

"I'll get dressed right now. Give me 15 minutes." She hung up the phone and got ready.

When Bobbi got to the coffee shop, she was in a world of panic. What could have happened? She didn't know Howard that well yet and didn't know if this was something abnormal or not. It did kind of scare her a little and make her question who she was involved with.

"Thanks for meeting me, Bobbi. Let's sit down."

"Are you okay? You have me scared to death!"

"I'm so sorry, honey. It's a long story. I need $15,000 tonight and don't know what I'm going to do." He told her.

"What? Howard, what are you talking about? This is crazy. What do you need that kind of money for?"

"I owe my bookie for some bad bets. I tried to collect the money that your boss owes me, but he won't pay. I'm in some serious trouble here, and if I don't come up with that money quickly, I don't know what Lenny will do to me." He explained.

"Oh my God Howard. How could you get mixed up in something like this? What do you mean Mr. Fitzgerald owes you money?"

"It's a long story, sweetie, we just have to figure out how I'm going to get this money. You want me to be around, right baby?"

Bobbi felt lost. She wanted Howard around more than anything. She found him mysterious and attractive, and no man had ever made her feel the way he had. But this was crazy! She barely knew this man, and already he was showing her another side of him that could put her in danger. *Why am I always choosing the wrong men?* Bobbi thought to herself.

Bobbi agreed to help Howard find a way to pay his bookie, but had a terrible feeling about the whole situation. Was she getting herself in way over her head?

Chapter 4

The next day, on her way to the firm, Bobbi couldn't stop the flood of thoughts going through her head. What they had decided to do last night was crazy. How could she be considering such a thing? They were talking about setting up her boss, stealing money, possible murder, and several other crimes she never even thought she was capable of. Her head was spinning.

Howard and Bobbi had stayed up all night devising a plan that seemed fool proof. He told Bobbi to do her small part and he would take care of the rest. It was that simple. Howard didn't want her to know any of the details. She just needed to listen to him and everything would be okay. They would be together, maybe even forever, if this worked out, he told her.

"Good morning, Mr. Fitzgerald," Bobbi said as she walked into the office. Howard had told her to avoid mentioning the fact that she was having a relationship with him, so her boss wouldn't become suspicious.

"Good morning, Bobbi. I have some documents being dropped off by carrier before noon, so please make sure to wait to take your lunch until then. I will also be leaving around 3 o'clock today to have an early dinner with Mrs. Fitzgerald, so I will need you to close up shop for me."

"Of course, Mr. Fitzgerald." *This is perfect*, she thought. With her boss gone earlier than originally thought, she would be able to start going through the files that Howard needed without any distraction.

Just then the phone rang. She picked it up, "Mr. Fitzgerald's office."

"Bobbi?"

"Yes?" "It's Howard. I need you to listen very carefully. You need to go into old Fitzgerald's office and open up his filing cabinet. You have the key, right?" He asked her.

"Yes, of course, Howard. But, can't I wait until after 3 when he plans to leave?"

"No. I need you to do this now. Remember baby, no questions. Just do what I say okay?"

Bobbi knew this was the time to change her mind. Although she was an independent woman in a conservative society, she was no criminal. What was she thinking? This could ruin her life! She could lose her job, or worse, end up in jail! Her parents and friends would want nothing to do with her if this ever came out. But, on the other hand, she was attracted to the danger of it all. They would be talking about her for generations. She would finally be more than an "old spinster." Maybe this was the true act of independence she had been waiting for.

"Of course, Howard. I'm going to the office and will call you back when I have the documents." She hung up the phone and looked around.

Bobbi checked to make sure that everyone was at lunch before she decided to go into Mr. Fitzgerald's office. The carrier had already come and gone with the documents he needed, so there was no chance of interruption.

She entered the office, and put the key into the filing cabinet. Once again, she looked around to make sure no one was approaching. She opened the drawer, and found the file marked "Personal. Inside the file, she found what she needed, and closed the drawer. Howard would be so proud of her, she thought. He would make sweet love to her tonight for her efforts. Just the thought of him kissing her was getting her excited.

Bobbi had to hurry to make copies of the items in the file and replace them before Mr. Fitzgerald returned from his lunch. While she waited for the copies, she began to look at what was in the file. *Oh my God! Can this be true?* This was much more serious than she thought. She was involved in some bad business right now and it was looking like it was going to be too late for her to get out.

Hurrying back to the office, Bobbi almost ran right into Mr. Fitzgerald. "Oh my goodness, Mr. Fitzgerald. I'm so sorry. I wasn't expecting you back so soon."

"I decided to come back early so I wouldn't be behind, since I have to leave so early today. Is something wrong Miss Brooks?"

"No, of course not. Why do you ask?" Bobbi replied.

"Well you are sweating and look as white as a sheet."

"Oh, I'm sorry, I feel like I might be coming down with a cold." She told him nervously.

Bobbi couldn't sit still for the rest of the day. She had to return that file to the cabinet before there was a chance that Mr. Fitzgerald found out about it missing.

Just when Bobbi thought she couldn't take it any longer, Mr. Fitzgerald decided to leave for the evening. Thank goodness, she thought.

"Goodnight, Mr. Fitzgerald."

"Goodnight Bobbi, try to finish those documents before you go ok?"

"Sure, tell the Mrs. I said hello."

Bobbi quickly looked around to make sure no one saw her, and headed into Mr. Fitzgerald's office. She unlocked the filing cabinet, just as someone startled her. "Bobbi, what are you doing?" Mr. Fitzgerald asked her.

Oh no, he was back. What did she do? What could she say? *Think quickly Bobbi, don't blow it.* She told herself. "Oh my goodness, Mr. Fitzgerald, you startled me. I was just checking to make sure I locked the filing cabinet earlier when I was filing some of the billing statements."

"Oh, ok, well goodnight." He replied, and left the office.

That was close, too close, she thought. Bobbi needed to get the paperwork and get it delivered to Howard without any more problems. She hurriedly finished up her work and headed out to meet him.

Chapter 5

"Did you get it baby?" Howard asked her.

"Yes, Howard, but we need to talk." Bobbi replied nervously.

"What about? You're not having second thoughts are you baby? I need you."

"Not necessarily second thoughts, but I'm not sure what you have me involved in here." She said.

"Baby, we said no questions, remember? You have to trust me." He pushed her hair away from her face.

"Then why am I copying files of financial statements and pictures of women who are tied up and blindfolded?" Bobbi asked.

Howard seemed agitated. "I told you, James Fitzgerald is not a nice guy, baby. You shouldn't have looked at those pictures."

"Who are those women?" Bobbi asked him.

"Don't worry about them, I will explain later, for now, let's have some fun." Howard said, as he kissed her neck.

Detective Charles Brower couldn't understand why these murders were getting to him so much more than the others. He felt a connection with these women that he hadn't felt before. It was like he was responsible for them. He was their voice. He had to solve these crimes for them, so they could rest in peace.

"I just can't understand why the bodies are being dumped in popular places in Hollywood," said Detective Brower. "It seems like the murderer is trying to tell us something through the locations." He told his partner, Hugh Fenton.

"I mean, The Pantages, The Roosevelt, Grauman's, The Farmer's Market. The locations have to mean something." Said Brower.

"It does seem strange that the bodies would be dumped in such public places at such well populated times," said Hugh.

"I can't sleep, I can't eat, I can't even spend time with my wife, until this case is solved, Hugh."

"I understand, buddy, but you can't let these cases run your life."

As the men stood at Farmer's Market, waiting for the coroner to finish taking pictures, something dawned on Charles Brower. There were 12 murder victims in all, all dark haired beauties, all young, all slender, and very sensual looking. But that wasn't all, he realized. All of them had a famous first name. There was Betty, Joan, Mae, Judy, Carol, Myrna, Marilyn, Marion, Jane, Doris, Lucille, and Ava. They all shared the first names of famous actresses!

"That's the connection, Hugh. They are all famous first names."

"Oh great, Brower, what are we supposed to do, guess which actress comes next and find every dame with that name?" Hugh asked.

"I don't know, but that has to be the connection. There is a pattern. Now how do we follow it and stop it?" Brower replied.

Detective Charles Brower was a 35-year old married man with two kids. He and his wife Shirley had been married for 10 years, and were so happy it made others sick to be around them. Charlie and Shirley were high school sweethearts, and always knew they would end up together. He worked hard, sometimes too hard for Shirley's liking. He missed ball games, parent conferences, and an occasional dinner party with his wife because of work. But, solving crimes was what Charlie was passionate about, and he felt he owed the victims his help.

Charlie lived to see his family. He was just about to walk in the door with roses for Shirley when his radio went off. He ignored it thinking if it were important, they would just call him at home. Just then Shirley came outside and told him he had a phone call. "Charlie, you have a call honey, it's the station. Are those flowers for me?"

"Yeah baby, I missed you today. How are the kids?" He replied.

"Come in and see for yourself, dinner's on the table."

He put his things down on the table, and picked up the phone. "Smells great, babe. Detective Brower here." He spoke into the phone.

"Brower its Gardiner. You better get down to The Knickerbocker fast, there's another body here." The Captain explained.

"Oh no, I just walked in the door and was sitting down to dinner...alright, I'll be right there." Captain Gardiner wouldn't have called the house unless it was important to the case, so Charlie wasn't about to delay.

"Charlie? Seriously? I mean, this is the third time this week." Shirley said. "Oh, never mind honey, just go solve this case quickly, so we can see you again." She gave up trying to nag him a long time ago.

With that, he kissed Shirley and was on his way.

Chapter 6

Bobbi couldn't believe she was so infatuated with this man. The danger of him turned her on. She worried she was making a mistake by getting involved with him, but didn't want to think about that right now. She was having too much fun.

"Baby, could you please get me a cigarette," he asked.

"Of course, darling I will be right there."

Howard was out on the small patio of Bobbi's apartment making some notes about their plan for the day. Bobbi wanted to know nothing more than she had to. What she saw yesterday really shook her.

"We have to get going soon honey, we need to meet my friend Roger for lunch." Howard told her.

"What happened with the money situation, baby? Did you pay your bookie?" She asked.

"Not yet, that's why we're meeting Roger."

"Ok, I'm ready." They headed out of the apartment.

On their way to meet Howard's friend, they stopped for some cigarettes and snuck into a local lounge to have a cocktail. They needed to relax a little.

After heading out of the lounge, they drove downtown to a small area just outside of Chinatown. They pulled over to the curb and waited.

"What are we waiting for, Howard?"

"My friend, sweetie, I told you that." He said with hostility.

"Well why can't we meet him at the restaurant? I'm starving."

"I told you to stop asking questions, remember?" He responded with a tone that she didn't recognize.

Bobbi didn't like the way he looked at her. This was the first time she remembered him being condescending toward her. *Who does he think he is?* She wondered. *I mean, sure we all know it's a man's world, but I'm an independent woman, which is why Howard was attracted to me in the first place, right?* She shrugged it off for now.

Just as she was about to make her peace with him, a man with a topcoat and fedora came walking through the darkness. He seemed to be walking very slowly, constantly checking behind him, to make sure he wasn't being followed, she noticed.

He approached the driver side of their car and said hello to Howard.

"Hey a Howie. How's it goin'?" The man leered at Bobbi.

"Fine Roger, we've been waiting for over a half hour for you. Why are you late?" Howard asked him.

"Just some other business to take care of, you know how it is."

"Let's just get this out of the way, ok?" Howard told the man.

"Alright, alright. Who's the dame?" Roger asked.

"Bobbi."

Bobbi didn't like the way Howard introduced her either. Why hadn't he said, my girl, or this is Bobbi, my friend? It was so curt and unlike him.

"Ok, Howie, here's the money you need. I need it back by next Thursday at 8 p.m. or we're all gonna be in trouble, capisce?"

"Yes, I got it. See you Roger."

With that Howard and Bobbi sped away down the street on their way to dinner.

"Where do you want to eat baby?" Howard asked her, acting as if nothing had happened.

"Howard, who was that man? Why are you borrowing money from him? What is going"…before Bobbi could finish her sentence, Howard slapped her right across the face. She was speechless, and in a fog. Did he really just slap her? She thought. She opened the car door and began to get out, still a little light on her feet.

"I don't think so hon. I told you to stop questioning me." He grabbed her and pulled her back into the car.

"Who the hell do you think you are! You can't hit me!" Bobbi screamed.

"Baby, don't make me hit you again. I really don't enjoy it." He told her calmly, as he held her arms down.

What had just happened? She was on her way to dinner with a handsome man, not 10 minutes ago, and out of nowhere, he just slapped her across the face. After he dropped her off, she told herself she was done with Howard Starks forever. She vowed she would never allow any man to put his hands on her…ever.

"Baby, don't be mad. I can't have you asking me all sorts of questions about things you wouldn't understand. It's for your own good." Howard told her.

Bobbi didn't even respond. She didn't know what to say. She thought he might hit her again if she said the wrong thing.

"Basically babe, here's the situation. I owe a lot of money to my bookie, and quite a few other people. I steal from Peter to pay Paul, so to speak. It's very complicated, but if you don't cooperate and help me do whatever it takes to make the money, and pay off these people I owe, I'll expose you to your boss. It will be a big mess to explain, since he has a part in this too." He told her.

Bobbi began to feel sick. "How did this happen? Poor judgment with a man and now she was being blackmailed? How many women made poor choices with men? This was her punishment for trying to have a little fun? What was she going to do? How was she going to get out of this?" She wondered. Bobbi couldn't believe this was happening to her.

Howard dropped her off at the door, of course without walking her in, and told her to be ready at 8 a.m. tomorrow. The gentleman routine was over.

Bobbi walked into the apartment, sat down, and began to sob. How did she get herself into this mess? She felt sick. Should she telephone someone? Should she get into her car, leave town, and never come back? Her family would find out and she would never be able to see them again. She couldn't take the chance of Howard and his "friends" harming them. Who was he involved with? Was he just trying to scare her into participating in his little crime spree? Bobbi had to talk to someone, get some advice. But, who could she turn to?

Chapter 7

Detective Charlie Brower pulled up at The Knickerbocker Hotel about a quarter to nine. He jumped out of the car and ran over to the area that was taped off. His partner, Hugh was already at the scene. "What happened Hugh?" Charlie asked.

"Well, it looks like the same M.O. as the previous victims. The girl was blindfolded and gagged and dumped out here on the street. It's a damn shame. She's gorgeous just like all the other ones." He replied.

"Anyone know her name?" Charlie asked.

"No, we're working on identifying her now." Hugh told him.

"I'm going to canvas the area and try to get some information from any witnesses. I'll be right back. And, Hugh, no one gets on the scene without seeing me first."

"No problem, Charlie. Take your time, man."

Charlie walked the block taking in the street. There were too many people out. It was going to be hard to find a witness who actually saw something they thought was strange. Hollywood was a strange place anyway. Most people tried to mind their own business, and tended to turn the other cheek for fear of being involved.

Just as he passed the coffee shop on the right, he ran into a man and his girlfriend, who were arguing. As he approached, they seemed to stop talking. "Good evening, folks."

"Hello there," the man said.

"I'm Detective Brower of the L.A.P.D. and I was wondering if I could ask you a few questions."

"What about, sir?" The man asked.

"Well there is a girl we found murdered back by The Knickerbocker, and I thought maybe you saw or heard something?"

"No, detective. We didn't see anything." The man said, a little too quickly.

"Are you sure, because to be honest, when I approached you both, I overheard you talking about the hotel." Charlie told them.

"No, really, we didn't see anything, detective," said the young lady.

"Well, ok then, it looks like I'm going to have to ask you both to come down to the station to answer some questions then." Charlie began to motion for them to come with him.

"Oh, Joe, just tell the man what we saw," urged the woman.

"Alright, detective. My girl here and I were walking down the block just having a chat, when a car pulled up and two men ran inside the hotel. They looked a little suspicious, so we decided to rest a bit to see what they were up to."

"And then what happened?" Charlie asked.

"They came out carrying a long bundle. It almost looked like a large rug or something. Ginny and I thought it seemed a little strange that they would be carrying something like that out of the hotel. We thought maybe they were stealing it or something. They were kind of looking over their shoulders to make sure no one was paying attention to them, and they seemed like they were in a hurry."

"What happened next? Where did they go?"

"Well they carried the bundle to their car and then sped off around the corner. That was the last we saw of them, and nothing else seemed unusual until we came back about a half an hour ago and saw the lights."

"Can you describe the men? How many of them were there?"

"I think there were three men, right Ginny?" He asked his girlfriend. "They were wearing black trousers, and black coats. They also had on black hats and were fairly little guys. I'd say that two of them were about 5'3 and the other about 5'5."

"Anything else you can think of that might help us out?" Charlie asked him.

"Oh, wait," the man remembered. "One of the men had a birthmark on the top of his forehead, shaped like a map of Italy."

"Ok, thanks so much for your help folks. I know many people don't like to get involved in a situation like this. I really appreciate your cooperation." Charlie didn't feel right about this. He headed back toward the scene to review his findings with his partner.

Charlie walked toward Hugh. "Well I got some information and a possible description." He said.

"Oh, good, because I'm not having much luck here," said Hugh. It's like people don't want to help out for fear of someone targeting them." The whole boulevard is silent.

"Yeah, I've noticed that. It's strange though, the people usually want to help us solve these crimes."

"Not this time, my friend." Hugh replied, as he shook his head.

Something wasn't right with these murders. Charlie had a bad feeling that the worst was yet to come.

Chapter 8

Just as Howard promised, he was there to pick Bobbi up at 8 a.m. He no longer cared about the efforts he put forth to be a gentleman. He simply honked the horn for Bobbi and sat in the car. What a jerk, Bobbi thought. She began to feel sick and had to run to the powder room. When she emerged, Howard was pounding on the door.

"Damn it, Bobbi, answer the door!" He screamed.

"I'm coming, Howard." She called after him.

She ran to the door, opened it and he looked as though he might hit her. "What the hell are you doing in here? Didn't you hear me downstairs?"

"I'm so sorry, Howard. I haven't been feeling well all morning and was in the bathroom."

"Well let's go, before I make you feel worse. We're late."

He basically dragged her to the car. Once inside, he began to tell her what was going on. "Listen now Bobbi. I'm gonna tell you a little bit about what's happening. You see, these men I'm involved with don't like women too well. Or maybe, they like em' a little too much, if you know what I mean. They like to have some fun with these 'ladies,' then get rid of em'."

"What are you saying, Howard? Are you talking about murder?" Bobbi asked.

"I'm not talking about anything, but you need to know there are quite a few men in this town who love spending some time with women, then don't want others to know about it. One of them is your precious boss, Fitzgerald. He likes the raven-haired beauties, I assume it might be because his wife is a redhead? He also likes it a little rough, if you know what I mean."

Bobbi felt sick. "What are you talking about Howard?"

"Oh, Bobbi, you're a smart girl, figure it out."

Bobbi couldn't believe her bad choices. Not only was she caught up in this, but now she found out that her boss was a cheater, and worse, possibly a murderer?

"What exactly do you want from me Howard?"

"I'm getting to that." He turned back to the road.

They pulled up to the front of The Knickerbocker Hotel. "What are we doing here?" She asked.

"Just get out of the car and be quiet, Bobbi."

They got into the elevator and stood silent all the way up to the 7th floor. Once they exited the elevator, Bobbi got a terrible feeling. They headed down to room 710. "When we go in, you need to be quiet and sit with me," said Howard.

Knock, knock, knock. "Yeah, who is it?" A voice called out.

"It's Howard, Moe let me in."

The door opened and Bobbi was ushered inside. Once inside the dark, musty room, she was told to sit on the bed. "Who's your friend, Howard?" The man referred to as "Moe" asked.

"This is Bobbi. She'll be helping us out for a while."

"Oh good, I like her. You know I have a thing for blondes. Can't wait to see her later." Moe looked Bobbi up and down, in a way that made Bobbi want to vomit.

Just then the door to the adjacent room opened. A man who was balding, had dark glasses, and a slight accent came into the room. "Howard, who is this beauty?" He asked.

"Hi-ya boss. This is Bobbi. She's going to be of great service to us." Howard told him.

"Hello sweetheart. You sure are a looker. I'm so glad you'll be helping us out." The man said as he kissed the top of Bobbi's hand.

She was about to ask the man what exactly she would be helping out with, when the door to the adjacent room opened again and three girls were forced into the room. All three girls were blindfolded and had their hands tied behind their backs. All of them were brunette, slender, and tall—about 5'7 or so. "What the hell is going on here?" Bobbi asked with panic in her voice.

"Damn it Bobbi, I told you to be quiet," Howard scolded her. He grabbed her aggressively by the arm and made her sit on the bed.

The three girls started to cry, and began to beg for mercy. "Please help us, whoever you are. We don't know what these men want," cried one of the girls.

Bobbi couldn't stand to watch this and not help these women. She almost vomited right there on the carpet. She had to get out of there. She began to run toward the door, when Howard grabbed her and pulled her back. "Where do you think you're going sweets? I told you to sit down and be quiet."

She sat back down on the bed, and tried to keep calm. The girls continued whimpering and Howard began sizing each one of them up with the man he called "Boss." "What do you think, Boss? Which one will the client like?" Howard asked.

"I'm not sure Howie, that's why we have three pieces of ass here. Call him up and ask him to come down to the hotel and he can choose which broad he wants. Make sure to tell him that this time, he cleans up his own mess!"

This has to be some type of forced prostitution. Bobbi thought. She wasn't naïve, but hadn't been around anything like this before. If the girls weren't being forced to prostitute themselves, why the blindfold and ties? A million thoughts were running through Bobbi's mind. She knew at this moment that she was in way over her head this time.

Howard got on the phone and called someone. "Yeah, the girls are here. You need to get down here now to pick one out. We got a room for you. Boss says any funny business this time and you clean up your own mess, got it?" The person on the other end of the line hung up abruptly and Howard put the phone down.

He motioned for Bobbi to follow him out of the room. They were leaving. In the elevator, Bobbi looked over at Howard. "Why are you involved in this Howard? You seem like you have so much more to offer."

"Listen baby, you don't know anything about me and I'm making a damn good living by arranging dates for friends." He said.

"That's what you call this? It looks to me like you're more of a pimp." She said.

"Yeah, you're probably right, sweetheart, but I like to think of myself as part of a larger corporation. I'm the head executive." He sneered.

"Why are those girls tied up?"

"What'd I tell you about asking questions?" He thought about it and then responded, "I guess it wouldn't hurt to tell you that they have been, hmmm, how do I say it,…lifted from their homes, cars, and other places." Howard told her.

"Are you telling me these women have been kidnapped?"

"That's another way to put it---yeah." Howard told her.

"Oh my God Howard, what have you gotten me involved in?" Bobbi cried.

Chapter 9

Charlie woke up exhausted. It was only 4:30 a.m. and still dark outside. Shirley was sound asleep next to him. Poor Shirley, he thought. She's so patient and puts up with way too much from me. Who would want this life? He wondered. Any other woman would have probably given up and left him, or had an affair on him by now. But, as the years went by Shirley stayed loyal and supported him through the tough times.

This case was driving him nuts. He couldn't remember letting any case affect him as much as this one had. What was it about these victims? Of course, he had to be a voice for the women, but maybe it was that they were all so beautiful, naïve, and full of potential? They were all the types of girls you would take home to Mom. The kind of girls who could be your sister, or your girlfriend. These were girls who didn't deserve the type of death they were given. The worst part about it, was that they reminded him of Shirley. That scared him. It hit a little too close to home. That had to be it. That was the reason he was so involved in this case. The girls reminded him of his own wife. Charlie felt sick to his stomach.

He had always felt like Shirley was too good for him. Although they had been together since high school, there was something unattainable about her. She was that girl everyone wanted to date. She was pretty, popular, and had a great laugh. The boys just melted around her. The way she could tell a joke made everyone smile.

Charlie and Shirley had been neighbors their entire lives. They lived across the street from one another, but hadn't spent much time together since they were kids. One day, on the way home from school, Charlie walked up the street to find Shirley crying on the curb outside her house.

He wasn't sure whether to approach her or not, but did anyway.

"Hey Shirley, are you ok?" He asked.

"Oh, Charlie Brower, what do you care for? You boys are all alike, you just want one thing," she responded.

Charlie didn't know what to say or do, so he just sat down on the curb with her and listened. She went on, "I was asked to the Homecoming Dance by George Davies. So today, we were going to look at some flowers and get ideas for our date. Well, as soon as I got into the car, he tried to get fresh with me and wouldn't take no for an answer. I had to literally pry his hands off me. He got upset and told me to get out of the car. So I had to walk home." She cried.

"He made you walk home? What a creep. You know what, I'll go take care of him." Charlie told her.

"No Charlie, just leave it alone. He's not worth it. Thanks for listening though."

"I'm sorry Shirley. I'm sure you'll find another date. You probably have tons of guys waiting to ask you to the dance."

She wiped her face. "What about you, Charlie? Are you going to ask someone to the dance?"

"I haven't really thought about it."

"Well, why don't you ask me?" She asked.

Charlie thought he must have misunderstood her. There was no way that Shirley O'Neill was asking him to ask her to the Homecoming dance.

"What do you mean?"

"I mean, why don't we go together Charlie? You could ask me, you know."

Charlie thought about it for a minute. "Well, would you want to go to the Homecoming Dance with me Shirley?"

"I'll have to think about it," she said. "Just kidding! Of course, I'd love to go with you."

Charlie couldn't believe his luck. In the past 20 minutes, everything had changed. He was taking the most popular girl in school to the Homecoming dance! "Sounds great Shirley. I have to get going for supper, but let's talk tomorrow about the details."

"Sure Charlie. Thanks for asking me. I'm excited to go with you."

From that moment on, Charlie and Shirley were inseparable. They spent the remainder of their junior year together, then stayed together through senior year, and finally got married a few years after high school. Charlie felt like the luckiest man on earth every day that he looked at his charming wife.

There were times when he looked at her, though, that he thought she deserved much more than him. She was intelligent, witty, stunning, a great mom, and had many friends. She always tried to do what was right and was very routine. Maybe too routine. Their relationship at times lacked excitement. It wasn't just that they had been together for over 10 years. She was just a little shy about trying new things, especially in the bedroom. It was hard for him to "convince" her to spend some time with him under the sheets. It was rare that she didn't have a headache. He missed the intimacy he had with his wife early on in their marriage. He was lonely and a little frustrated. Charlie often wondered why Shirley didn't try to make him happy in that way. He thought he deserved a little more effort on her part.

It was time to get to work. No more thinking about the problems in his marriage. It was time to focus on the case. This case was the only thing keeping him going like a deranged animal every day. He had to find the killer before more innocent girls had to die.

On the way to the station, he stopped at the local newsstand and picked up a copy of the Times. The front page was plastered with photos of the crime scene at the

Knickerbocker. Great. Just great. How am I supposed to explain this to the Captain? Charlie thought to himself.

Heading into the station, one of the desk sergeants stopped him. "Hey Brower, did you read the front page? They're saying you have no clue where to start with these murders."

"Thanks for that, Sam. We're working on it. You know the press."

"Brower! Get into my office, now!" The Captain screamed at Charlie.

Great. He was in for it now.

"Yeah Cap?"

"What the hell is going on with this case? This is getting way out of hand. I mean, press pictures of the crime scene! Who was handling this last night?"

"I'm sorry Cap. I have no idea how they were leaked these photos. The scene was secure and no one was around. Hugh and I were there the entire time. We're making progress though."

"This case is turning into an embarrassment to the department. You have to do more than make progress. You need to solve it. The public is getting uncomfortable." The Captain said.

"The public is getting uncomfortable? How about the girls and their families are getting uncomfortable."

"Watch it, Brower. Don't give me any crap. I need you to fix this so the department looks alright."

"Of course, Captain. I know the department doesn't want to look bad."

"Watch it smart ass. Just make sure you do your damn job." The Captain walked back toward his desk, as Charlie shut the door.

Charlie knew he shouldn't give his boss a hard time. He was just doing his job and trying to make sure the department didn't look bad. This frustration over the case, his marriage, everything was starting to get to Charlie. He needed to go get a cup of coffee and think things over.

"I'll be back, Hugh," He told his partner. "Hold down the fort for a while."

Chapter 10

Charlie walked into Carolina Pines and sat down at the counter. "Coffee and a slice of cherry pie, please," he said to the waitress.

"You got it, hon." The waitress winked.

Things were getting out of hand very quickly. He needed some new developments or clues in this case. He had definitely hit a stand still. He couldn't live with himself if this killer wasn't caught, and soon. It would be his biggest regret. Charlie looked up to grab the cream. When he did, he locked eyes with the most beautiful woman he had ever seen. He could not turn away and found himself getting a little hot around the collar.

Wow, he thought. What great eyes. He hadn't seen her here before and Charlie knew most everyone around this block. She looked a little preoccupied. She was drinking her coffee very slowly and seemed to be in a fog.

"Excuse me, waitress?" She called.

"Yes, doll, what can I get ya?"

"More coffee please, and a slice of that cherry pie that he's having, please." The woman responded.

Charlie looked over at her. She seemed a little frazzled, almost so involved in her own thoughts that she didn't realize anyone else was in the diner with her.

Charlie was surprised by his feelings. He needed to talk to her. He hadn't looked at another woman this way since he had met Shirley. Why was he so attracted to this woman? He wondered. He should get up and leave right now before he said something he would regret.

Instead, Charlie felt himself rising from the barstool, and heading toward her. "I couldn't help but notice, that you seem a little bothered by something. Is everything ok?" He asked her. Where was that coming from? He thought. Oh, great. Now she was going to tell him to mind his own business.

She looked up innocently, and asked, "Excuse me?"

"Oh, I'm sorry, I don't mean to pry, it's just that you seem like you might need someone to talk to, is all." Charlie said.

"I do? Well I will have to be more careful about how I look, I guess." She shut him down right away. Clearly she wanted to be left alone.

Ok, I guess this conversation is going nowhere, Charlie thought. Nothing to worry about here. He tried to make friendly conversation and the woman seemed like she would rather eat rocks than talk to him. He turned to go back to his seat, just as she spoke.

"I'm sorry," she said. "I'm just having a very bad morning. I didn't mean to take it out on you. My name is Bobbi, Bobbi Brooks. And you are?"

"Charles Brower, but please call me Charlie."

"Nice to meet you, Charlie. I'm sorry again for coming across a little short."

"That's ok. I didn't mean to sound nosy, just thought you might need a friend."

"To tell you the truth, I do. More than you could know." She said.

The pie came, the coffee kept flowing, and Charlie and Bobbi spent the day in the coffee shop. They had so much in common, and found it extremely easy to talk to each other. The hours flew by. Charlie had never met someone whom he found so intriguing and attractive. Bobbi was classy, educated, and interested in him, to his surprise. They laughed, she touched his knee every so often, and he wanted to see her again. He was feeling excitement for the first time in a long time.

She asked about his wedding ring. "So, you're married? All the good ones are always taken."

"Yes, I have been married about 10 years to my high school sweetheart. Things have become a little strained and complicated lately, but that's marriage."

44

He's coming on to me, Bobbi thought. He was married, but she didn't care. She was so attracted to him. He had a smile that was so genuine. His eyes told of his pain and sacrifice, which made her want to find out much more about him.

They continued to talk for the rest of the afternoon, then Charlie suggested they take a walk around the park.

"That would be lovely," Bobbi said. "Shall we go then?"

The park was about a mile away, so they decided to take Charlie's car. He opened the car door for her and noticed her long legs. He felt guilty right away and found himself getting hot again.

Once inside the car, Bobbi began having second thoughts. Isn't this how she got involved in this situation with Howard? She needed to stop making quick decisions and be more cautious. Charlie seemed so sincere though, and he had really made her feel valued today in the coffee shop. Bobbi hadn't heard from Howard in about a week. He seemed to be done with her services. He had discarded her like a cheap piece of trash. She hoped he wouldn't bother her again, but had a feeling the opposite was true.

Charlie knew he shouldn't be spending time with this woman. He was feeling himself get excited by her. With everything going on in his life, he needed a break, and Bobbi seemed to come along at the perfect time.

They headed to the park, while continuing their conversation. Charlie found out a lot about Bobbi. She worked at a law firm, had never been married, and was looking for Mr. Right. She was so gorgeous. He couldn't stop staring at her lips, and he began to imagine kissing her.

Bobbi couldn't stop staring at Charlie, and wondered, *is he ever going to kiss me?*

They arrived at the park, got out and began walking. Once they had talked for what seemed like hours, it was time to go. Charlie hadn't been back to the station all day.

He told Bobbi he was working on the murder case she might have read about in the papers. He needed a break from it all today. She knew which case, and was worried about him. He seemed so tired. It was crazy that she was so worried about this man who was a complete stranger to her.

As they got back into the car, Charlie leaned over and kissed her passionately. She returned the favor and they began to embrace. Bobbi felt herself getting warm and tingly all over. She wanted him right then. Charlie wanted to rip off her clothes and have his way with her. "Bobbi, I want you, baby. Where can we go?"

"My apartment. It's just about 2 blocks from here."

Charlie put the car in drive and they drove silently to Bobbi's apartment and headed inside. They both knew they shouldn't be pursuing this, but couldn't help themselves.

Once inside, Charlie began to kiss Bobbi, and removed her sweater. She started to touch him, he became excited and they landed on her bed. Bobbi felt like this was a dream. She couldn't get enough of him. She was ready to feel him, when he began to take off his pants. "Charlie, I want you, baby."

Afterward, they lay together, smoking. "That was amazing, doll."

"Yes, it was Charlie. I'd love to see you again. Can we make this work, somehow?"

"I really want to baby, we will have to take it day by day for now ok?"

"Sure Charlie, whatever you feel comfortable with. I just want to see you." Bobbi felt like she was on cloud nine.

Charlie left the apartment after kissing Bobbi goodbye. He promised to see her again soon.

When Charlie returned to the station, he had three messages from Shirley. *Shit. I can't believe she called three times. I better come up with something good to tell her.* He thought.

Charlie picked up the phone and dialed the house. Shirley picked up the phone on the first ring. "Charlie?"

"Yeah, baby, what's wrong?" He asked.

"I went to the store this morning and had this terrible feeling I was being watched. I decided I didn't want to finish shopping, and left the store. When I came home, I saw a man in a Chevy pull over a few houses behind ours. He just sat in the car and didn't get out. I looked out the window, and he drove by the house a few times really slowly and just stared. It frightened me, Charlie."

"Well I'm on my way, baby. Just lock up the house and sit tight." He told her.

Charlie felt horrible about today. Not only had he cheated on his wife, but she was scared to death because some creep was following her. If anything ever happened to her, he couldn't live with himself. *What a schmuck I am. Out running around with some other woman, while my wife was looking for me to protect her.*

He grabbed his things, ran out the station door, and sped home.

Chapter 11

"Hello?" Answered Bobbi.

"Hi ya Bobbi. I need a favor." *Oh no*, she thought, *not again.* It was Howard. Bobbi felt herself getting sick. She hadn't heard from him in about a week, and she was beginning to hope she never would.

"Howard, I'm exhausted. I've been running around at work all day and need a break."

"Hey doll. How about you don't try to tell me when you're tired. I tell you what to do." He said curtly. "I need you to meet me at 7:30 tonight down at the diner."

"Fine, Howard. What do you need me to do?"

"Don't ask so many questions. I will explain when you get there." He hung up the phone.

Bobbi got dressed and left her apartment. She wanted to stop and pick up some cigarettes at the liquor store before she headed to the diner. *Why won't he just leave me alone,* she thought. *What more does he want from me?*

Bobbi arrived at the diner about 10 minutes early. Howard was nowhere to be seen so she sat at the counter. "Coffee please," she asked the waitress. She couldn't stop shaking and felt a panic attack coming on.

There was a man sitting in the back booth staring at her. She couldn't see his face because of the way the lighting was casting a shadow on him. He was smoking a cigarette and looking right at her. He made her uncomfortable, though she didn't know why.

Howard came into the diner and made eye contact with her. "Let's go, doll. We have things to do," he motioned for her to leave.

Once again, Howard let her open her own car door. No more chivalry. This was business. She got into the car and asked Howard where they were going.

"Down to the Roosevelt. We have a meeting with the boss and another client."

"Why do I have to go, Howard? I don't want any part of this." She pleaded with him.

"Because baby, don't you see, the girls feel much more comfortable with you there. They think because you're a woman, you'll help them or will prevent any harm that may come their way."

Bobbi felt sick. A thought crossed her mind. Maybe she could tell Charlie what was going on. He would protect her. He was the police. That was what she needed to do. He would take care of everything.

They got to the Roosevelt and Bobbi felt like she was going to throw up. Every time she had ever been to this beautiful hotel, she had a fantastic time with great memories. Now, she would forever be reminded of the horrible things she had to be a part of here.

They took the elevator up to room 205 and knocked on the door. "Boss, it's me," Howard said.

The door opened and Howard pushed Bobbi in. Howard's "boss" was eyeing Bobbi like she was full of butter and he'd like to eat her up right there. "Well, Bobbi, so glad you could join us again sweetheart." The man smiled.

"It's not like I had any choice." She replied with an attitude.

"That's why I like her Howard. She's sassy."

The attached door opened and once again the girls came in. There were three of them, this time blondes, with large breasts. They were blindfolded just like last time and had their hands tied behind their backs.

"Why are you doing this to us?" One of the girls screamed.

"Hey baby, be quiet, will ya?" Howard said in response.

"Ok, here's the deal, Bobbi. This time we need you to go downstairs and get the client, bring him up here, allow him to pick which girl he wants, then leave him alone with her," explained Howard's boss.

Bobbi couldn't stop staring at the girls. Howard slapped her across the face. "Got that Bobbi?" Howard asked.

"What? You bastard! You can't just hit me! I can't believe you're making me be part of this! The girls began to cry when they heard Bobbi's opposition to the plan.

"Sorry, sweetheart. You are involved, and I don't want to have to hurt you any more than I already have." Howard told her. "Now, you're scaring the girls here, tell them everything's alright."

Bobbi knew there was no way out of this. If she went downstairs and didn't return, they would just come looking for her. "Fine, let's get this over with so I can go home."

Howard followed Bobbi downstairs so he could keep an eye on her. Bobbi went into the bar and ordered a vodka tonic. As soon as she sat down, a man who looked to be in his late 30's approached her. "Hey baby, can I buy your drink?" He asked.

Bobbi didn't even turn to face the man. "No thank you. I'm waiting for someone. I appreciate the offer though."

"Well if you're looking for some fun, you should give me a shot."

Oh, geez, what a creep, Bobbi thought. Not only did she have to sit here acting like she was enjoying herself, but this loser wanted to make a pass at her.

"Look, I don't mean to be rude, but I already told you I'm waiting for someone."

"I know, baby. I think you might be waiting for me. You're Bobbi right? I'm Sam. Can you take me up to see the product now?"

Bobbi suddenly became very nervous and didn't know what to do. Was this the guy? How did he know her name? She wondered.

"Sure, I'm sorry Sam. I had no idea it was you. I apologize for not accepting your drink offer."

"No problem baby. How could you have known?"

He followed Bobbi upstairs and once they got to the room, Bobbi knocked three times as instructed. The door opened and Howard came out. "Go on in, Sam. Bobbi will show you the goods." Bobbi looked at Howard with daggers in her eyes.

They sat down at the table and Bobbi introduced the girls. The poor girls were still bound, but their blindfolds were removed so he could see them. All three appeared to be slightly drugged. They weren't crying or shaking as they were when Bobbi had left them. "What do you think, Sam?" Bobbi asked the man. It was hard for her to even get the words out, she felt so nauseous.

"What are their names?" Sam asked.

"Carole, Marilyn, and Dorothy." Bobbi told him.

"This is tough, but I think I'd like to spend some time with Marilyn there."

"Ok, girls let's go. Sam, just knock when you two are done." Howard told him.

Bobbi exited the room and had to run to the bathroom. She couldn't hold it in any longer. This was disgusting and she was helping to exploit these poor girls!

Howard told her she could go, and she walked home, crying the entire way. She was in some real trouble. *How will I get away from these men?* Bobbi thought. By the time she reached her apartment, she had a plan.

Chapter 12

About 2 a.m. the phone rang. Charlie picked it up and got dressed quickly, before he woke Shirley. "Charlie where are you going," Shirley asked.

"I'm sorry baby. I have to go, another body's been found."

"But Charlie, I'm nervous to be alone after what happened today." She pleaded with him.

"Don't worry sweetie. I will have a patrol car come park outside for the night. You'll be safe." He said. He kissed her on the cheek, grabbed his jacket, and left the house.

Charlie felt bad leaving her, but he had to take care of his case. Were his priorities a little mixed up? Probably, but he had a job to do.

He drove over to Hollywood and Vine where the body was found. He pulled up to the scene and was instantly fuming. "Get these god damned people out of here!" He yelled at one of the officers. "They're on my crime scene! What the hell do I have to do to get people to follow protocol around here? Amateurs!"

"Hugh, what the hell is going on here? Why is no one keeping these people off the scene?" Charlie screamed.

"I just got here Charlie. I don't know where our backup is."

"What do we have this time?" Charlie asked.

"Another young woman. Looks to be in her early to mid twenties. This time, though, the woman is blonde. She has ID on her. Says her name is Marilyn Claussen. She's 5'5 and about 115 pounds. Real pretty too." Hugh reported.

"Super. Another girl with an actress's name. I knew this was a pattern. Somebody had to see something. Where are our witnesses?" Charlie asked.

"That broad over there says she heard screaming about 12:30 or so coming from the alley. When she went to check it out, she couldn't see anything." Hugh replied.

"Well, let's start with her," Charlie said. "We'll regroup in about 20 minutes after I check out the scene."

"Alright, sounds good." Hugh said.

Charlie lifted the crime scene tape and began to walk the scene. There wasn't much to look at. The poor girl was lying on her back in the middle of the sidewalk. She was wearing just a white bra and panties. She had tearstains on her cheeks where her mascara had run down her face. She had gorgeous, light blonde hair, and full, beautiful lips. Her complexion was flawless. She had milk and honey skin for sure. Strangely, she wasn't wearing any jewelry. No ring, necklace, earrings, or bracelet. Most women didn't leave their house without their jewelry. But, she was in her panties and bra, so maybe it was removed.

The poor girl died with her eyes open. She was shocked. The way she looked up at Charlie broke his heart. He closed her eyes gently with his fingertips. He couldn't bear to have her look at him while he processed her as just another crime scene. He didn't feel that way, but he had to detach himself somehow, or he would never see things clearly enough to solve this damn case. He had already been warned by both the Captain and Hugh that he was getting too close. Once that happened, you became soft. You couldn't see the evidence anymore. He just couldn't help it. These girls were dying and it was his fault. He had to solve these murders before anyone else lost their life.

"What happened to you sweetheart?" Now he was really losing it. He was talking to the dead girl. "Marilyn, help me find this man who did this to you." Charlie was becoming more and more frustrated every day. They just couldn't seem to catch a break. The killer was starting to get much bolder, less inhibited. The bodies were turning up on public streets rather than in private locations. *How can a body be dumped right here on the boulevard without someone noticing?* He wondered.

"What do you think, Charlie?" Hugh asked him.

"I think it's a damn shame we aren't making any progress on this case. The only thing we know is that they all share first names with famous actresses. We thought he liked dark haired or brunette girls, but now we have a dead blonde. I can't see the pattern and it's driving me crazy."

The body was removed and taken to the morgue for further investigation. An autopsy would have to be performed and her family would need to be notified. The pictures of the dead girl would be in the press before tonight's paper run. Damn press. All they did was cause more problems for the cops. Charlie had this aching feeling that he needed to call Bobbi. He knew this situation with Bobbi was not right and that he could be risking everything, his wife, his family, even his career. But, right now, she was the only thing that gave him any sense of a break from his miserable life.

By the time Charlie got back to the station, it was 9 a.m. He looked up Bobbi's number in his notebook and called her.

"Hello," she answered on the fourth ring. "Hey Bobbi, it's Charlie."

She smiled. "Oh, Charlie, I was hoping you would call. I've been thinking about you a lot."

"I've been thinking about you too. Can I see you today?" He asked.

"I have to work pretty soon, but we can meet for a quick lunch if you want."

"That sounds great. I have some paperwork to do and I will meet you at the coffee shop about 1?"

"I'll be waiting, darling," Bobbi said. And they hung up.

Bobbi couldn't wait to see Charlie. He gave her butterflies that she couldn't explain. He was handsome, smart, sarcastic, and a law man. But, he was married and had children. Why did she keep getting involved like this? Sure, she was an independent woman, but did she need to get involved with dangerous or unattainable men to prove it? No one could say she wasn't getting what she deserved. Maybe it was time she grew up and made some changes in her life, or things could get much worse.

Chapter 13

After getting to the office, Mr. Fitzgerald called her in and asked her to shut the door. "Bobbi, I don't know what kind of involvement you have with Howard Starks, but I would suggest you stay away from him."

"Why do you say that, sir?"

"Let's just say I had some business dealings with him and he proved to be a shady character."

I'll bet, Bobbi thought. After what she saw in the file in Mr. Fitzgerald's office, she knew he was part of Howard's little "service."

"Thanks for the warning, Mr. Fitzgerald. I don't really know him, and haven't seen him since that day he came in looking for you." She lied.

"Oh, I'm glad. I was worried for you. Just looking out for you darling." Fitzgerald said.

Oh you're looking out for me alright, she thought. *More like, you're worried about your little secret being exposed. What a creep. I can't believe I have to work for a man who is involved in all this.*

Bobbi moved her thoughts to Charlie. She couldn't wait to see him, even if it was for just an hour. She locked up her desk, grabbed her keys, and headed out to the coffee shop. It was a beautiful day out, so Bobbi decided to walk the three blocks. On the way, she caught a glimpse of the Los Angeles Times. The headline read "Blonde-Haired Beauty Found Dead on Hollywood and Vine." Bobbi stopped to read the article and felt sick. She thought she might pass out right there on the street. The blonde woman in the picture was Marilyn from last night!

Oh my God, Bobbi panicked. *What do I do now?*

Bobbi had to run to the alley where she got sick. She didn't know what to do. She was going to tell Charlie all about Howard and this little prostitution/kidnapping ring that he had going, but now she was involved in a murder? How could this happen? She wondered. Could she be put in prison for her part in all of this? She couldn't face Charlie right now with all of this going on. She would have to stand him up and call him later telling him something came up. She just couldn't make sense of all this right now.

Charlie was waiting for Bobbi for over a half an hour and began to wonder if she was going to show. He didn't know her well, so he didn't know if this was unusual or not. She seemed so anxious to meet him though. Strange. Maybe something came up, he thought. He would have to get back to the station and would call her later. He needed to check on Shirley soon anyway.

Back at the station, Charlie and Hugh racked their brains for a connection in the case. The phone rang.

"Coroner on line 1 Charlie," Hugh called.

"Brower here."

"Hi Detective Brower, it's Dr. Ford. I've been looking over the autopsy results from the last few girls you brought in and I found something a little strange."

"What is it Dr.?" Charlie asked.

"There appears to be a tooth missing from each of the girls dental cavities."

"What?" Charlie didn't think he heard the doctor correctly.

"It's really strange, but it looks as though someone yanked out one of each of the girls' teeth, maybe as some type of souvenir?"

"Oh Christ. This just keeps getting better and better. Thanks for getting back to me so quickly Doc."

Charlie hung up the phone and stared at it. "Why would someone want teeth?" He said out loud. What type of sicko was he dealing with here? He picked up the phone to call Shirley and check on her. He also needed to tell her he wouldn't be home for dinner…again.

She picked up on the first ring. "Hey baby. How are you doing?" He asked.

"Oh, Charlie I'm so glad it's you. Can you come home a little early tonight? I don't really want to be alone with the kids right now." He could hear fear in her voice.

"Oh, sweetie, I was just calling to check on you and tell you I had to work late."

Silence.

"Shirley?"

"Yeah, Charlie?"

"Baby, what should I do?" He asked.

"Just get your work done. I will speak to you later." And with that, she hung up the phone.

Great. Just what he needed. More guilt. Because he didn't have enough of it right now. His heart was telling him to go home and spend time with his family. The case would wait. He needed to be there for Shirley. The other part of him said, stay and finish your work. These murders need to stop. No wonder so many detectives were divorced. It was tough balancing both family and a job that never stopped.

Charlie stayed at work and called Bobbi. She answered. "What happened to you today, Bobbi?" Charlie asked.

"Oh, Charlie, I'm so sorry, I got held up at work and couldn't reach you."

She sounded funny. Something wasn't right.

"Are you ok, doll? You don't sound right."

"I'm fine. I'm just a little preoccupied. I've got a lot on my mind lately." She told him.

"Anything I can help with? I would love to see you for a bit."

"I wish I could Charlie, but I'm exhausted and was just getting ready for bed." She was seriously sick with nerves and couldn't imagine going anywhere or seeing anyone.

"Ok. I understand. It's been a tough day for me too. If you change your mind, call me at the station. Have a great night, Bobbi." He hung up the phone.

Bobbi was glad he didn't press the issue. She felt bad for telling him no, but she was in big trouble and didn't want to involve him. Her life was a complete mess and she had no one to talk to about it or help her out of this hole she had created. These patterns had started early with Bobbi, and she never seemed to grow out of them. The past couldn't be undone, but you'd think she'd learn from her mistakes by now.

Chapter 14

Bobbi was an only child. Both her parents spoiled her rotten, thus she got anything she wanted. Always. Because of this, she was constantly bored. If you can have or do anything you want, what fun is that? That's where Bobbi got into trouble. She was ditching school in the 5th grade, going instead to the local soda shop for a milkshake. Her mother would get a call from the Principal, head down to the shop, and drive her back to school.

In middle school, Bobbi began "dating." It was really just necking with the boys after school in the parking lot. They might go to dances together occasionally, but it was more about experimenting and finding out what felt good. Bobbi's parents seemed to give up on her in middle school, so from then on, she pretty much did whatever she wanted.

Once Bobbi entered high school, she was in heaven. She had never seen so many attractive boys. They were all filling out, lifting weights for football, and flirting with her every day. She couldn't keep her mind on her school work. All she could think about were the boys and which ones she would date that weekend. Bobbi didn't have a bad reputation, necessarily. She dated a lot, but didn't go all the way. It was mostly about the kissing, maybe letting the boys get to 2nd base. She never wanted others to see her as scandalous or "loose." She wanted to have fun and enjoy her school years, but didn't want to be known as the town floozy either. One thing she learned from her mother was to protect her reputation, because it was all she had.

During her senior year of high school, Bobbi started dating Curtis Goldman, the cutest boy in school. He was tall, good-looking, funny, sweet, and the captain of the football team. Curtis had a swagger that everyone loved. Bobbi wondered how she got so lucky. She had the perfect boyfriend, and made it her mission to find out what he was hiding. No one could be that perfect, she thought.

Months went by and everything was going well for Bobbi and Curtis. He treated her like his princess and mentioned marrying her. Bobbi wanted to wait until graduation to begin talking about marriage. She felt she was still too young to settle down. She loved Curtis, but marriage was way down the road.

In January Bobbi missed her period. February came and still nothing. She began to panic. Could she be pregnant? They had been so careful. She had to find out. Bobbi went to the doctor by herself after school one day. She was 18, so she didn't need her parents to go with her. She knew by the look on the doctor's face that she was in fact pregnant. She began to cry her eyes out right there in his office.

Bobbi left the office in a fog. What was she going to do? She couldn't tell her girlfriends or it would be all over town by the end of the day. She had to talk to Curtis, but what would she say? "Curtis I'm pregnant and I don't want to be?" He would be crushed if she didn't tell him right then and there that she was ready to marry him and raise a family.

The next day, Bobbi met with Curtis on the bleachers after school. She told him about the pregnancy and he was so excited. He told her they could get married right away and start their lives together. Bobbi wasn't so sure. She just stared at him. Curtis asked her what was wrong. Bobbi told him she wasn't ready for marriage and a baby, that she wanted to go to work, and be single for a while. He looked at her as if she were a foreign creature. What type of girl wouldn't want a baby and marriage? It was the life all girls desired.

After hours of discussing it, Bobbi informed Curtis that she would be having an operation to get rid of the baby. Curtis could not support this and told her that she was not the girl he thought she was. He broke up with her right then and there. Bobbi was crushed. Just because she wasn't ready to have a baby and marriage didn't mean she didn't love Curtis and want to be with him.

For days, Bobbi called and pleaded with Curtis to take her back. She told him she loved him and couldn't live without him. He told her the only way they could get back together was for her to have the baby and marry him. Bobbi couldn't accept that.

Bobbi had the operation, and no one knew. Curtis didn't take her to the hospital, and didn't call her afterward. In fact, he never spoke to her again. She had to make up some grand story at school as to why they broke up, but the rumor was that Bobbi cheated on him. He refused to speak on it to anyone.

Once the rumors started, Bobbi figured she might as well make them true, so she began to date a lot of boys. Again, she never slept with them, but she got around a little. She started going for the bad boys. The more mysterious, the better. She liked the boys who smoke, drank, and drove motorcycles. It was exciting for her to be part of their world. They couldn't promise her happiness like Curtis did. She never knew from day to day what kind of trouble she could get into. She liked the mystery of it all.

Once high school graduation came and went, Bobbi got the job in the law firm and had worked there ever since. She never really had many girlfriends because she had some trust issues. She didn't want anyone ever to know all of her business. She could take care of things on her own, just like she had in school.

Bobbi never heard from Curtis again after high school. She always wondered what her life would have been like if she had had the baby and married him. She would obviously be a much different person, but would she like her life? She sure as hell wasn't liking it now.

Bobbi was scared to death about what was to come next. She had a sinking feeling that Howard would call again.

"Damn it, Howard. How are we going to keep covering these problems up for him?" Howard's boss asked.

"Sam isn't going to take the fall for this one, Boss. He says he never saw the girl again after he left the hotel around 11." Howard replied.

"Yeah, right, just like the last one. If he isn't the one doing this, then who is?"

"I don't know, but maybe we should cool it on the service for a while, you think? I'm worried about loose ends coming down on us." Howard said.

"Yeah, you're probably right about that. Call the clients and let them know we're taking a little break, and they would be wise to lay low."

Chapter 15

Bobbi barely got any sleep that night. She was tormented by nightmares about what she had seen. *Why didn't I help those girls?* She thought. *I could have helped a girl stay alive if I had only been brave enough to go to the police. That poor girl, Marilyn. The way she was discarded on the street like that was awful.* Bobbi couldn't believe she had just seen the woman alive twenty-four hours ago. She made up her mind that she was going to tell Charlie what was going on in the morning. She had to take responsibility for her part in all this and do it before more damage could be done.

That night, Charlie returned home to find Shirley waiting in the family room in the dark. "Charlie, are you having an affair?" She asked him.

Oh no. She suspected something. Should he come clean and tell her or lie?

"Shirley? Why are you sitting in the dark sweetie?"

"Answer me, Charlie." She had been crying.

"Sweetheart, what on earth are you talking about?" He felt horrible for making her feel like she was crazy to suspect him.

"You know damn well what I'm talking about, and I'm going to give you one chance to tell me the truth and that's it." She said.

"Baby of course I'm not having an affair. Where are all these ideas coming from?"

"I just feel like something is wrong. You're different. Our marriage is different. You don't try to touch me anymore. You don't call to check on me or the kids. I feel like I don't know who you are lately."

"I'm so sorry Shirl, it's just this damn case. It's really getting to me, you know?" He went and sat next to her on the couch and put his arm around her.

"I love you and the kids more than anything. I just have so much pressure on me at work and I'm not handling it very well. I promise I will start making a much better effort to include you in what's going on."

"Alright, Charlie, but you know if something is bothering you, you have to talk to me. I'm your wife, I love you, and don't want us to have any secrets from each other. Once people start lying to one another, the marriage falls apart. I watched it happen to my parents, and don't want the same to happen to us."

"We aren't your parents baby and we won't fall apart. Now, let's go to bed." They went into the bedroom and made love like they hadn't in months. Charlie hated to lie to Shirley, but promised himself he would not have any more contact with Bobbi Brooks and would do everything it took to make Shirley and the kids his first priority.

Charlie woke up the next morning feeling refreshed. He was ready to start over with everything, the case, his marriage, everything. He was feeling much better and couldn't wait to make some progress today. He would call Bobbi this morning and tell her he had made a mistake and had to work on his marriage. She would understand.

On his way into the station, he ran into Hugh. "Hey partner. I've been thinking a lot about the case and have some ideas. Do you want to meet in about an hour to go over them at the coffee shop?" Hugh agreed and they decided to meet at Carolina Pines.

"Wow, Charlie it looks like you're doin' better today?" Hugh told Charlie when they slid into a booth at the diner.

"Thanks, Hugh. I had some clarity last night on the case and I'm ready to catch this bastard."

For the next hour, Charlie and Hugh discussed everything about the case. They had overlooked some important items. How could they miss these? Some great leads were beginning to pop up and it looked like they were on their way to making an arrest.

On the way back to the station, the men stopped for a copy of the morning paper. The cover read, "No New Leads In Hollywood Murder Case." "Just what we need. More press," Hugh commented. "I wish they could do us some good for once."

"Maybe they can, Hugh. I think I have an idea."

"Well what exactly has you so excited, Charlie?" Hugh asked.

"The coroner says that he found missing teeth from each of the girls' mouths when performing the autopsies. It looks like the perp is taking one from each as a type of souvenir."

"What? Well that's a new one. We haven't seen that before."

"So, we need to start figuring out what connection someone might have to the girls and why he might want a souvenir of the killings."

Just as Charlie was about to continue, he noticed Bobbi walked toward them. She radiated a glow that made him stop in his tracks. She looked up and made eye contact with him, and continued walking toward the men. Just as they approached one another, Charlie stopped and said, "Hello Bobbi. This is my partner Hugh Fenton."

"Nice to meet you Hugh. I was just on my way to get something to eat around the corner," she replied.

Charlie took the opportunity to tell her he'd walk her back to the coffee shop. "Hey Hugh, I'll catch up with you in a few." His partner just smiled and continued on to the station.

"Are you ok Bobbi? You look exhausted." Charlie asked her.

"I'm fine. Just a rough day at the office. So that was your partner?"

"Oh, Hugh. Yeah, we're brainstorming on the case. You might have seen something about it in the *Times*?"

"I did as a matter of fact, and I need to talk to you about it. Do you think you could come by my apartment around six today?"

Charlie felt torn. He promised himself he was done with Bobbi, but was curious about what she could offer to the case. "Sure I can be there Bobbi, but what exactly is this about?"

"Just meet me and I'll fill you in ok Charlie? Thanks. I'll see you then."

She walked off so quickly that Charlie couldn't argue with her, so he turned and headed back to the station.

Chapter 16

Six o'clock came and Charlie was knocking on Bobbi's door. No answer. He waited a few more minutes and knocked again. Nothing. A neighbor walked by and asked Charlie if he was looking for Bobbi. "Yes, we had an appointment at six, but it seems she stepped out."

"I saw her go into her apartment at 4:30 and she hasn't left. I've been downstairs on the stoop since then," said the woman. "You know, we've all been worried about her the past few days. She is normally such a jovial girl, and lately she's been down, depressed, and hasn't been eating at all."

"That's strange. I only met her a few days ago, but she seemed fine," Charlie added.

"Bobbi is one of the friendliest people I know, but like I said the past few days, she's been someone I haven't seen before."

That's really strange, Charlie thought. *She specifically asked me to meet her here at six o'clock today right?* Maybe he misunderstood. He would go down to the payphone and call Hugh to see what he could work on tonight instead. Just as Charlie was about to leave, he stopped. Something didn't add up. She got home at 4:30, didn't go anywhere, and wasn't answering the door. Bobbi had also been very depressed lately. He was replaying the conversation in his mind. *No, it couldn't be*, he thought. This was crazy. He had that feeling though that something was very wrong.

Charlie knocked again, and once again no answer. He decided to kick the door in. Once he did he saw Bobbi lying unconscious on the floor next to an empty bottle of sleeping pills. "Oh my God! Bobbi! Wake up!" He shook her.

Charlie ran to the phone and called for an ambulance. "This is Detective Charlie Brower and I need an ambulance at 210 3rd street immediately!"

Charlie rode in the ambulance with Bobbi on the way to the hospital. Why would she do this? What was going on with her? Charlie had to admit that he didn't know her well enough to even guess what had happened to her to cause harm to herself. Had she wanted him to find her?

At the hospital they whisked Bobbi away and began pumping her stomach. Charlie took the time to call Shirley. "Hey babe, I'm gonna be stuck a while. How are things going with you and the kids?"

"Things are really good, Charlie. The kids are having dinner and will be going to bed soon. Take your time. I'm fine sweetie."

"Kiss them goodnight for me and I will see you later."

Charlie hung up the payphone and went to the front desk. "Can you tell me how Bobbi Brooks is doing? They just took her back to pump her stomach."

"She's fine sir," the receptionist said. "They were able to revive her. You can see her in about an hour."

"Will she be released tonight?" Charlie asked.

"No, any suicide attempt requires a 72 hour hold for observation." The receptionist replied.

Perfect. Charlie was going to have to wait around to speak to her when they were finished admitting her. This wasn't how he planned on getting work done tonight. He went down to the cafeteria to get a cup of coffee while he waited.

About an hour later, Charlie returned to the desk. "Can I see her now?"

"Yes, Detective Brower you can go in now. She is in room 209," the receptionist told him.

Charlie walked into the room and his heart broke for her. Bobbi had looked like a mere shadow of herself. She was pale, had large dark circles under her eyes, and an IV in her arm. Poor girl, he thought. Why would she do this to herself?

He sat with her for a while and watched her sleep. Even after what she had been through, she still looked beautiful, almost angelic. Charlie thought it was odd that no one had come to see her while she was in the hospital. Where were her family, or her friends? Maybe there was a lot more to Bobbi Brooks then he knew.

"Charlie?" She whispered.

She was coming to. "Yes, Bobbi, I'm here," Charlie responded.

"What happened? Where am I?" She seemed very confused.

"You don't remember doll? You're in the hospital. You tried to hurt yourself."

"What? No! What are you talking about?"

"You swallowed a whole bottle of sleeping pills."

It was still a little fuzzy but was starting to come back to Bobbi now. "I didn't try to hurt myself, Charlie."

"But sweetheart, I found you on the floor next to a bottle of pills. You had taken twenty or more pills."

"Charlie, I need you to believe me. I did not take those pills. Someone forced me."

"What are you talking about? Why would someone try to force you to take sleeping pills?"

Bobbi knew she should tell him the whole story right then and there, but was feeling so weak, she didn't want to get into all the details. "I need some rest, Charlie. Please believe me. Be patient with me and I will tell you the whole story."

"Alright Bobbi. You get your rest. I'll be here when you wake up. I'm just going to go call into the station and grab a bite and I will be back." *What's going on here,* Charlie wondered. *Why would someone try to harm Bobbi?*

"What happened with the dame?" Howard's boss asked.

"I took care of it." He replied.

"I need you to be a little more specific than that Howie."

"Let's just say I paid a little visit to her apartment and she's taking a long nap."

"We don't want any loose ends here Howard. There is way too much at stake with these murders all over the papers."

"Don't worry boss. I took care of it. She won't be a problem anymore I promise. Nothing to worry about. All loose ends tied up, except for Sam of course." Howard said.

"What the hell are we going to do about Sam?"

"Nothing for now, boss. Nothing we can do. No one can find him."

Chapter 17

Bobbi woke up and saw Charlie sitting next to her. "Hey there," he said. "How are you feeling?"

"Better. I'm just a little groggy. When can I check out?"

"You can't just yet. They're keeping you for observation. They want to make sure you're alright."

"Charlie, I'm fine. I didn't do this to myself. I wouldn't try to kill myself. You have to believe me!"

He could see she was starting to get really upset. "Ok, ok honey. Of course I believe you, but why would someone try to harm you?"

"Look Charlie I have something to tell you and I don't know how, so I'm just going to start at the beginning."

Bobbi started at the beginning of it all. Charlie just sat and listened. "A man came into my office about two weeks ago, and asked to see my boss. My boss, Mr. Fitzgerald was visibly upset by this man's visit. The man's name is Howard Starks."

Charlie wrote the name down in his notebook. He looked up at her for her to continue.

"Well, anyway, this man, Howard came back the next day and Mr. Fitzgerald wanted nothing to do with him. He started to come on to me a little, and I was interested. He asked me to lunch, so I went."

"Let me stop you for a minute, Bobbi." Charlie continued. "Did he get to see Mr. Fitzgerald the day he came in and took you to lunch?"

"No, he didn't seem interested in seeing him any longer. He just came to take me to lunch. We went to lunch and things were going really well. He asked me to dinner for the following night, and we began dating."

"Time for your medication hon," the attending nurse said.

"What exactly am I taking?" Bobbi asked

"Just a little something to make you sleep."

"I can sleep fine. I don't want anything."

"I'll let the doctor know, sweetie." The nurse left.

"After we began dating, he called me in the middle of the night, clearly agitated asking me to meet him right away. I went, against my better judgment, and things have been bad ever since."

"What do you mean, Bobbi? What did he want you to meet him for?" Charlie asked her.

"I didn't know at the time, and to tell you the truth, I'm still not sure how I fit into all of the plans, but he basically told me that he needed my help paying off some gambling debts."

"Ok, so then what happened," Charlie asked.

"Pretty soon he became forceful and began ordering me around. He also hit me when I wasn't doing what he asked. He told me I had to help him or I would be in trouble, because I snooped through some of Mr. Fitzgerald's files."

"Why didn't you go to the police right then?" Asked Charlie.

"I was afraid. I didn't want to lose my job, and I wasn't sure how much trouble I would be in."

"What exactly did you do, Bobbi? What would you be in trouble for?"

"I'm getting to that." She continued.

"So finally he calls me up one night and asks me to meet him at the Roosevelt. I told him I didn't want to be involved and he told me he would be at my apartment to pick me up, no excuses."

She stopped for a moment to catch her breath. She continued. "I went with him to the Roosevelt, and was ushered up to one of the rooms. When we got there, there were three girls who were blindfolded and had their hands tied behind their backs. I was scared to death. I had no idea what I was getting into."

"Wait a minute! These girls were bound and blindfolded? Bobbi didn't that ring any bells for you with the murders going on?" yelled Charlie.

"Charlie, please don't yell at me. This is hard enough for me to tell you. I didn't know too much about the murders at the time, I just knew what I was seeing wasn't right."

"Ok, I'm sorry, continue on." Charlie shook his head as he began to write down the details.

"So as I went into the room that night, I was told I had to go downstairs and get a man named Sam. I did as I was told and brought this man back upstairs. Once he got upstairs he chose which woman he wanted and I left. The next day as I was on my way to meet you, I stopped when I saw the *Times*. I almost got sick right on the street because the murdered woman was the woman Sam had chosen that night."

"Bobbi, you should have went to the police right away," Charlie told her angrily.

"It's a little more complicated than that, Charlie. I was involved with a detective, had criminals after me, and didn't want to end up in prison."

"Bobbi, I probably could have kept you out of it, but I can't guarantee anything now. You're in way too deep."

"I know that Charlie, and I'm not asking for any favors. I just don't want any other girls to die."

"I'm so sorry for everything you are going through. Are you saying that you think this Howard guy might have given you the pills?"

"Yes, that's exactly what I'm saying. I would not take pills, Charlie. Nothing is that bad. I know I have problems, but I take it day by day. I remember him calling me, and coming by to drop off a check, for what he said was 'my part.'"

"And that's the last thing you remember?" He asked.

"Yes, until I woke up here."

"Ok Bobbi, I don't mean to leave you alone, but I've got to get working on this. I will assign an officer to your room and you'll be safe. Please call me at the station if you think of anything else, or need anything at all," he called as he ran out the door.

Bobbi knew that what they had would never be again. She could see the look in his eyes that he could no longer be involved with her. She was fine with it. Her days of getting involved with married or dangerous men were over. She felt relieved she had finally told someone what was going on, and went back to sleep.

Charlie ran out of the hospital and hailed a cab to the station. His car was still at Bobbi's, so he would have to make arrangements to pick it up later. Right now, he had to tell Hugh about the new developments on the case and find this Howard Starks.

"Hey Hugh," he yelled as he ran through the door, find out everything you can about a Howard Starks. No known address, but search the Hollywood vicinity."

"Right away. Where have you been, anyway? Cap's been looking for you all day."

"I've got exciting news about the case, Hugh. We're on the edge of solving it, I can just feel it!" He said as he headed to his desk.

Charlie picked up the phone. He needed to check in on Shirley and the kids. The phone range five times, but no answer. *That's strange*, he thought. It was eight o'clock. *Where could they be?* Maybe she turned in early and didn't hear the phone ring. He would try again in an hour.

"I found information on this Howard guy, Charlie. Let's pay him a little visit huh?" Hugh said.

"Let's go." Charlie grabbed his coat.

They rode out to Franklin Street and ended up at some of the dumpiest apartments in the area. "He lives here?" Charlie asked. "This place is a dump." The worst criminals seemed to find the seediest dwellings.

"Let's head up and take a look." I'd love to see what we find up there," Hugh said.

Once they got up to the 7th floor, they found apartment 714. "Is this the place?" Asked Charlie.

"It's the last known address for the guy that I could find."

Knock. Knock. Knock. "Howard Starks are you in there? It's LAPD and we need to ask you some questions." Charlie called out.

No answer. They knocked again. Still no answer. "Alright, Mr. Starks, you give us no choice but to barge our way in."

"Ready Hugh? One. Two. Three!" The men barged through the door and secured the scene. "Nothing here," said Hugh. "I'd better check the bathroom."

Charlie looked around. What a dump. How sad it was that someone had to live this way. There were a few skin magazines lying around, some left over crumbs from a sandwich, and the television set was still on.

"Charlie, you better get in here!" Hugh yelled from the other room.

"What's up, Hugh?"

Charlie walked around the corner, to find what he presumed to be Mr. Howard Starks lying on the bathroom floor, dead.

"That's just great. I hate to sound cliché, but another dead end," Hugh said.

"Real funny, Hugh. How the hell are we supposed to move forward now when our only lead is dead?" Charlie felt like he wanted to crawl in a hole and sleep for days. Just when he thought they had a break, their only possible suspect was dead.

"I'll call the coroner," Hugh said.

"Ok, while we wait, let's look around this place and get anything we can to move forward. I want phone numbers, trash, schedules, etc. Anything we can use." Charlie told him.

While they searched, Charlie filled Hugh in on the woman they ran into and how she was connected to the case. The men spent the rest of the evening combing Howard Starks' apartment for evidence or clues, while Bobbi rested comfortably in her hospital bed.

Chapter 18

"Good morning, sunshine," Charlie said to his wife. "Where were you last night baby? I tried calling you about eight and you didn't answer?"

Oh, I took the kids for ice cream and we weren't back until around 8:30. How is the case going?" Shirley asked.

"We actually thought we had a big break last night, but our suspect ended up dead. This case is wearing me out. I can't remember one where I was so involved emotionally."

"Oh, Charlie. You're always like this. I hate to break it to you baby, but that's what makes you a good cop."

"Thanks Shirley. You always know how to make me feel better, babe. I'll see you later ok?" He bent down to kiss her before he headed out to pick up Hugh.

Charlie and Hugh were on their way to the hospital to see Bobbi. Charlie wanted to ask her some more questions now that Howard was dead. When they walked in the room, Bobbi was sitting up and looked much better than yesterday.

"Hey Charlie. How are you?" She asked.

"I'm good, Bobbi. You look much better than yesterday, that's for sure."

"Oh, thanks. I told you I had no intention of hurting myself. These doctors realize that and are just making sure I'm strong enough to get out tomorrow."

"Eh hem…" Hugh cleared his throat.

"Oh, I'm sorry, Bobbi this is my partner Hugh Fenton."

"Nice to meet you, ma'am."

"Hello, nice to meet you too, Detective Fenton."

"Let's get down to business, Bobbi. I don't want to scare you or anything, but Howard Starks was murdered," Charlie informed her.

"What? Oh no. How will you prove my story then? Does this put me in jeopardy?" Bobbi asked.

"Actually, Bobbi we think you will be safer now that he's gone, but it leaves us a little lost for clues." Charlie replied.

"Can you remember anything else about the past couple of weeks, that you didn't tell Charlie yesterday?" Hugh asked.

"Not really. I wish I had a name for Howard's boss, but he simply went by 'Boss.' As far as the other things go, I didn't get Sam's last name, but I might be able to describe him."

"Ok, we will get an artist in here to try to do a sketch. That's a good place to start. Hugh, why don't you go call the station and get someone down here to meet with Bobbi?"

"We'll do. I'll be right back."

After Hugh stepped out, Charlie told Bobbi he was glad she was feeling better and that he was sorry again for everything she had to go through. He also told her he couldn't continue their affair and felt really guilty about what he did. *Thank goodness*, she thought.

"Charlie, I feel the same way. I want to do things right. No more getting involved with unavailable men. I think I'm ready to start sharing my life with someone and it's time I stopped playing around."

Charlie smiled. He felt so relieved. There were no hard feelings between them.

Hugh walked into the room and Bobbi seemed to light up. "Hey Charlie, could you go find me some hot chocolate or something," she winked.

Charlie got the hint and headed off to check in with the station.

Bobbi and Hugh talked for hours. He told her all about himself and she did the same. The sketch artist came and went, and they lost all track of time. Bobbi couldn't believe how much they had in common. Charlie had already gone back to the station to work on the case, and left Hugh to watch over her.

The two of them really hit it off, and Hugh asked Bobbi out for a date.

Just as Hugh and Bobbi were getting comfortable, the night nurse came in and told Hugh he had a phone call. "I'll be right back, Bobbi."

Hugh picked up the phone in the hallway. "Detective Fenton," he answered.

"Hugh, it's Charlie. We have another body. I need you to meet me at Griffith Park right now."

"I'm on my way."

Hugh headed back to Bobbi's room. "I have to run, Bobbi. There's been another body discovered. I will be back in the morning to visit. Sweet dreams."

I can't believe how lucky I am. Hugh is a great guy. If something good can come of all this, it will all be worth it, Bobbi thought.

Hugh met Charlie outside the observatory. "What's going on Charlie?"

"We have another body. This time a redhead. Same build as the others and the same markings on the wrist. She was clearly bound."

"What else do we know about the scene?" Hugh asked.

"Not much. Same as last time. Body found without clothing, in her lingerie, eyes open as if in shock at time of death, ligature marks around her wrists."

"Ok, let's walk the scene." Hugh got out his notepad.

"Hey doc, can you open her mouth for me," Charlie asked the coroner.

"I'll be damned. Missing a tooth just like the others. Except this time it's the front tooth. That had to hurt like hell. Poor girl. Look at all that blood."

"Why would anyone want a tooth," Hugh asked.

"I don't know, Hugh, but we're not getting any closer to solving this case. I found an address at Howard Stark's apartment. Let's go check it out. It might be something."

They headed over to the Hollywood Hills area. The location was much more glamorous than Howard Starks' shabby apartment. The men wondered if this was a house that Howard has been casing for a possible robbery. The house was monumental to say the least. It was also absolutely gorgeous and had to belong with someone with a large cash load.

Charlie and Hugh pulled up the driveway, noticing the many expensive cars in front of the house. "Wow, someone knows how to keep a nice ride," Hugh said.

They continued on to the gate and dialed the house. A servant answered. "Hello, we're Detectives Brower and Fenton from the LAPD, is the owner of the house home?" Charlie asked.

"Yes, sir. Please pull forward and I will get Mr. Carlton for you."

Once they entered the residence, the servant had them take a seat in the living room and offered them a drink. "No thank you ma'am," Hugh responded.

When she stepped out to retrieve Mr. Carlton both Charlie and Hugh began to look around. There were some family photos, but the men didn't recognize anyone in them. Who was this guy? Why was his address on the table at Howard's house?

A stout man with tanned skin came into the room. He was smoking a cigar and looked as though he had been at the pool for the day. "Gentlemen, what can I do for you?" Asked Mr. Carlton.

"Hello, Mr. Carlton? We're Detectives Brower and Fenton from the LAPD. We'd like to ask you some questions about a case we're working on, if that's ok," Charlie explained.

"Of course. Ask away." He poured himself a drink.

"We're investigating a series of murders. Maybe you have heard of them, the Hollywood murders? There have been quite a few young girls found dead within the past two months."

"Yes, of course. I saw something about it in the *Times*," Carlton said. "I didn't know there were so many victims. Such a shame those beautiful girls in their prime had to die that way."

"Yes it is," Charlie said. "We've been looking into possible suspects for the murders, and a man, Howard Starks came up." Charlie waited to see if there was any reaction from the man. There was none. He acted as though he didn't recognize the name at all. *Maybe he doesn't know him, or maybe he's an excellent liar*, Charlie thought.

"Did you know anyone by that name, Mr. Carlton?" Charlie asked.

"No. Should I?" Carlton was a little too casual about being questioned. He was a pro.

"Well, we found him dead yesterday and upon investigating his apartment he had your address and phone number written down on a piece of paper," explained Hugh.

"Why would this man have my address and phone number if I've never met him?" Carlton asked.

"We were kind of wondering the same thing," said Hugh.

"Let me show you a photo of him." Charlie dug out the coroner's photo of the dead body. "You don't recognize him?"

"Jesus, Detective Brower. Do you really need to show me a photograph like that?" Carlton asked.

"I'm sorry it's the only photo we have of him."

"No, I've never seen that man before." Carlton looked away.

"What is it that you do for work, Mr. Carlton?" Hugh asked.

"Not that it's any of your business, but I'm an entertainment lawyer. I represent some high class clients in the entertainment industry. Now, is there anything else I can do for you gentlemen?"

"Nope, I think that's it for now. We'll be in touch." Charlie responded.

As the men walked back to their car, Hugh thought something was a little off. "He just seems way to casual about the whole thing, like he's hiding something. I don't trust him at all. Whoever this Carlton is, I have a feeling we're going to get to know him real quick."

Charlie agreed and they headed back to the city.

Charlie went back to the station and Hugh returned to the hospital to see Bobbi. *Good for them,* Charlie thought. *They seemed to be hitting it off.* After getting back to the station, Charlie did a little detective work on this Mr. Carlton. His name was John Carlton, III. He came from money. His father was an attorney who dealt with overseas and International clients. Both his parents had been married for 50 years before his mother died. His father was since deceased as well. He had a pretty normal childhood, nothing out of the ordinary. The only thing that looked suspicious was that John Carlton III had been arrested in his early twenties for soliciting. He was accused of being a pimp, basically. He ran a call girl service. *What? This didn't fit*, Charlie thought. *Why would a wealthy kid who turned into an attorney run a call girl business?*

Charlie had an unsettling feeling about John Carlton. He was going to ask around about him and find out what he could. The guy was a little too sure of himself, Charlie decided.

The phone rang. "Detective Brower."

"Hey Charlie. It's Hugh. I'm checking in. Any news?"

"I looked up some information on this Carlton character. It doesn't look right. He used to run a call girl business years ago. That fits with what Bobbi told us about the girls, right? I'm going to run a photo of him and bring it down to the hospital to see if Bobbi can ID him."

"Sounds great. I'll see you here." Hugh said.

"Speaking of Bobbi. You two are getting a little chummy don't ya think?"

"Oh, Charlie stop. I like her. She's sweet. I think it's about time I start thinking of settling down, don't you?"

"Yeah, Hugh. I do. You need someone to go home to."

The phone rang again. "Charlie, there is a man here to see you." It was Shirley.

"What do you mean, honey? Why would someone stop by the house to see me when I'm at work?" He wasn't paying much attention to her.

"I don't know. He says his name is Sam."

"What?" Charlie thought for a minute. "Jesus, Shirley get out of the house and drive anywhere you can!"

"Charlie, what are you talking about? Sam? Do you have a last name?" Shirley asked the man.

There was noise in the background, what sounded like the phone dropping, and the line went dead.

"Oh my God," thought Charlie, "the son of a bitch has Shirley!"

85

Charlie ran out of the station, calling for back up on his way to the house. He drove so fast, he nearly killed anyone in his path. He had to get to her. Who was this Sam? The same Sam involved in the case? What happened? Did he take her? All sorts of thoughts were going through Charlie's mind. If something happened to her he would never forgive himself. Maybe if he hadn't worked so much this wouldn't have happened. As Charlie screeched into the driveway, things seemed a little too quiet. Where was she?

Chapter 19

He saw the front door open and ran inside. "Shirley? Shirley? Are you here baby?" He frantically searched the house for his wife.

No answer. The radio was on, laundry strewn everywhere, it appeared she was in the middle of preparing tonight's dinner. She was no where to be found. Damn it! Charlie ran outside and went to the Brown's house next door. "Madge, did you see what happened to Shirley?" Charlie was frantic and was scaring his neighbor.

"No, Charlie. Why what's wrong son?" Madge replied.

"I think someone took her! She was on the phone with me and it went dead, and now she's missing!"

"Oh my, Charlie. What should I do?" Madge asked.

"Stay in your house with the doors locked. If you think of anything you've seen that was suspicious in the past week, call me immediately. In the mean time, can you get the kids after school and watch them until I know what's going on?"

"Of course, Charlie. You just let me know what I can do honey." Madge watched him run back to his car.

Just then Charlie's back up pulled into the driveway. The neighbors were starting to file out of their houses now curiously. The other officers walked around the neighborhood asking questions, looking for clues, while Charlie surveyed the scene. He couldn't look at his own house like a crime scene! He had to stay focused. He had to remain calm to help his wife.

Hugh ran up the driveway. "What the hell's goin' on Charlie? I heard you radio for backup and drove right over here."

"Shirley's missing! I was on the phone with her, when she said there was a man named Sam who was asking for me. She was telling me about him, when I heard something in the background, and then the phone went dead."

"Sam? Do you think it could be the same Sam that Bobbi was telling us about at the hospital?" Hugh asked.

"I don't know. But if it's not, that's a big coincidence."

"What should we do?" Hugh asked his friend.

"I couldn't handle it if something happened to her, Hugh. She is my life. We have to find her!" Charlie dropped his head into his hands and began to panic.

"Alright, Charlie. Calm down, buddy. We'll find her. I will put an APB out with her description, photo, and have every cop in the area looking for her. We WILL find her."

Charlie stayed with the other detectives to comb every inch of the house for clues. They found nothing. He had no idea what to do. He had never felt so helpless and disgusted with himself. He had a pit in his stomach and felt lost. This is what others felt like when something tragic happened to them. What was the next step? Charlie ran inside to throw up. How could he wake up tomorrow if they didn't find her? How would he explain this to the kids?

Bobbi was watching television when the news came on. *"Breaking news. A woman kidnapped from her home in Los Angeles around 2 p.m. today. The woman is Shirley Brower, Detective Charles Brower's wife, of the famed Hollywood Murders case."*

"Oh my God!" Bobbi yelled. The nurse came running, thinking she was sick or in pain. Bobbi pointed at the set and the nurse continued to watch with her. "Oh, honey, isn't that your friend?" The nurse asked.

Bobbi couldn't even speak. She just nodded. There was too much going through her head. Was she at fault for this? Why would someone try to harm Charlie's wife, unless it had something to do with the case? Could she have prevented this? Did she wait too long to tell someone? Would Charlie hate her for this? The phone rang. She answered without thinking. "Hello?"

"Bobbi? It's Hugh. Have you heard?"

"Yes, Hugh. Oh my God. Is Charlie ok?" She asked.

"To tell you the truth, he's not doing very well. I've never seen him like this. I really need you to do me a favor and try to remember anything you can about the past couple of weeks. I need to come by and show you a picture of a man we talked to today, and get any other information you remember on this Sam guy."

Oh no, Bobbi thought. *What did Sam have to do with this?* "Hugh, you think the man I met at the Roosevelt had something to do with this?"

"We're not sure right now Bobbi. I just really need your help. You might be the only person who will know how to find Shirley. I have to go, I will be by in about an hour."

Bobbi hung up the phone and began to shake uncontrollably. The nurse offered her a sedative. "No, I can't take anything right now. I have to think clearly to try to help." She told the nurse, and stared at the set.

Chapter 20

Shirley woke up and looked around the dark room. She had no idea where she was. She knew this man had given her something because she was really groggy. What was going on here? She wondered. This obviously had something to do with Charlie and the case, but why her? Why wouldn't they go after Charlie? All these thoughts were racing through her mind.

The room was about 10x10 and had solid black walls. There were no pictures or decoration of any kind anywhere, just a chair, a small bed, and an end table. There was also a telephone. Shirley picked it up. Of course there was no dial tone. What was the purpose of the telephone?

Shirley sat up on the edge of the bed. Her head felt like it was going to explode. She started to remember a little of what happened. The man wanted to see Charlie, but when she turned around to talk to him, he grabbed her and placed something over her mouth. She fought, and he finally hit her on top of the head. That was the last thing she remembered.

He must have hit her, then carried her out to his car? Where were the neighbors? Didn't anyone see me being carried out by a strange man? How did this happen, right in my own front yard? She wondered.

Shirley stood up slowly and tried to make it to the door. She knew it was probably locked, but had to try anyway. *Damn.* Of course it was locked. There were also no windows in the room, and just one light bulb hanging from the ceiling. It was freezing, and smelled musty. She had a hard time even standing up, but had to try to get out of this horrible place.

She tried knocking. "Hey, is anyone out there? I'm not sure why I'm here, or what this is about." She called out. She tried to remain calm. Panicking would only make things worse. Charlie had always taught her that if she was in a compromising situation, she had to stay calm, use her head, and get out alive.

No answer. She tried again. Knock. Knock. Knock. "Excuse me, sir? I'm Mrs. Charles Brower. I'm not sure why I'm here."

The door opened, and Shirley stepped back, startled. The man did not come in and she couldn't really see him in the darkness. He only placed a tray of food on the floor, slid it over toward her, closed the door and locked it again. Shirley started to panic.

"Hey!" She yelled. "Who the hell are you and what do you want?"

She looked at the tray of food, left it on the ground, and sat down on the bed, trying to work out some type of plan.

Bobbi couldn't sit still while waiting for Hugh. Finally an hour later, he ran through the door with some photographs. "Here, look at these. Do you recognize either of these men?" He asked her.

Bobbi looked at the photographs carefully. She only knew one of the men. "I know this one. This is Howard's boss, who seemed to be in charge of the kidnapping organization." Bobbi identified John Carlton III as Howard's boss. The other man had been a known acquaintance of both Starks and Carlton, so Hugh had to track him down in order to find clues to locate Shirley.

"Thanks, Bobbi. I'm so sorry you're involved in this, sweetheart. I wish I could stay with you, but we've got to do everything we can to find Shirley."

"Of course, Hugh. Please let me know what's going on. I'm sitting here in this hospital room worrying myself sick."

Hugh kissed her on the cheek and was on his way again.

The coroner called Charlie's office to let him know that the only other thing that he had to report from the autopsies of the girls was that they were all given some type of drug that sedated them for a while. The coroner reported that it was a type of barbiturate. Most often know as "reds" or "sekkies," these pills could knock someone out for anywhere from one to six hours. The women who were given these pills would have been really confused, groggy, and probably didn't have any idea where they were.

Charlie already figured the women had been drugged. From the description of the scene at the hotel that Bobbi had provided, along with the attempt on her life, there was no other explanation. The girls had been forced to do things against their will because they were drugged. Once the drugs kicked in, they were too tired to fight. Charlie had to find where the drugs were coming from. If he didn't work fast, he might never see Shirley again.

He knew this bastard had her. It had to be connected. Why would someone else want to harm her? He had to get some sleep, but felt guilty even shutting his eyes while knowing his wife was out there with some monster. Charlie needed to check on the kids. They had been staying with his parents since last night. He hadn't wanted to alarm them, so he told them their mother had to go visit a sick friend for a few days. He would check on them after he got a little shut eye.

Charlie walked down the hall to the break room, and turned off the lights. He took a spot on the comfy couch, sat down for a second, and he was out. Hugh was looking all over the station for Charlie. "I think I saw him go into the break room, Hugh," Detective O'Malley told him. "He didn't look good."

He opened the door and saw Charlie asleep on the couch. *Poor guy*, Hugh thought. *I wouldn't want to trade spots with him for anything right now.* Hugh decided to let Charlie rest, and closed the door quietly.

While Charlie rested, Hugh and the department worked on the case. Every man on the squad wanted to help. No one could do anything to help Charlie feel better, but they tried. They all felt like it could be their wives out there missing.

"Hey Hugh, I found some information on those drugs," O'Malley said.

"Great, let's hear it."

"Well, those drugs aren't used that often. They aren't real popular on the recreational scene. More people use them as a type of pain pill or relaxant." O'Malley explained.

"Ok, well that's a start, but find out what doctors are prescribing them, and how readily available they are. I want to find out exactly how many people have access to them."

"Will do Hugh. Oh, and Hugh, will you please tell Charlie that the guys are all sick about what's going on and we're here for him."

"I will buddy. Thanks." Hugh went back to work.

Charlie woke up in a panic. How long had he been asleep? He felt so groggy and a little nauseous. The pain and memories of what had happened came rushing back. With sleep, he thought maybe it had been a dream. No such luck. This was his life. His wife had been kidnapped and he had no idea where to start in order to find her. He sat up quickly, but thought he might pass out. When was the last time he had eaten something? Maybe yesterday morning? He wondered. He couldn't even think of eating, but felt awful.

He stood up a little slower and began to straighten up his shirt and tie. On his way out the door of the break room, he saw Hugh coming toward him.

"Hey Charlie, I was just coming to check on you, man."

"Hugh, how long have I been out?"

"Just a couple of hours."

"A couple of hours! Why didn't someone wake me? How could we lose two hours on this case?" Charlie yelled.

"Buddy, calm down. You needed your rest. The entire department is working on this. We've been doing everything we can. We're ordering some grinders and I wanted to make sure you were going to eat."

"I'm not hungry at all, but I'm feeling really weak."

"Well, you need to keep your strength up, for Shirley," Hugh added.

"You're right. Yeah, order me whatever you're having."

"Anything new since I fell asleep?" Charlie asked.

"Only some minor developments in the drugs that were given to the girls. We found out some more about the drug, how effective it is, and we're working on where it gets distributed."

"Thanks Hugh. To you and the boys. I appreciate all you're doing. I'd be lost without you guys right now."

"Charlie that's what friends are for. Now, come on, let's get you a grinder."

Time was not on their side, and the department was doing everything they could to find Shirley. The main question was, where was she and what was this bastard going to do with her?

Chapter 21

Bobbi had been pacing for what seemed like days. She had to get out of this hospital room, but couldn't leave until tomorrow afternoon. Why hadn't Hugh called her with an update? She felt so helpless in damn hospital room! Because of all the trauma she was being exposed to, they decided to keep her a little longer. She could be taking care of anything Hugh or Charlie needed right now. She also had to take care of work. She hadn't been to the office and needed to make sure they knew what was going on, before she lost her job. She picked up the phone.

The temp secretary for Mr. Fitzgerald answered. "Mr. Fitzgerald's office."

"Hi this is Bobbi Brooks, Mr. Fitzgerald's secretary. You are temping for me. Is he there? I need to speak to him."

"Sure Miss. Brooks, I will transfer you. One moment."

"Fitzgerald," he answered.

"Hello Mr. Fitzgerald. It's Bobbi."

"Oh my goodness. Bobbi! How are you sweetheart? We've all been worried sick about you. You got the flowers?"

"Oh, yes, thank you so much they are beautiful. I'm fine, sir."

"The hospital said something about you being on mandatory hold for a few days?" He asked, with a tone that suggested he was snooping.

"Not exactly, sir. That's the reason I was calling. I need some time off. Just a few weeks to get things in order. It's been a really tough week, and I need to rest."

"Of course, darling. You take all the time you need. We will be here when you're ready. In the meantime, I will have Miss Grainger, the temp write you a check for some sick pay."

"Oh, Mr. Fitzgerald. You're too kind, sir. Thank you so much. That would be a great help to me right now."

"Don't even think twice about it, honey. Can you come by tomorrow to pick up the check?"

"Yes, I will be there around 4. I will see you then."

"Ok, honey, have a good night. See you tomorrow." He hung up.

Wow, that was unexpected, Bobbi thought. Mr. Fitzgerald was a nice man, but never overly generous. Was this a whole new side of him? She wasn't going to question it. She needed the money and was grateful he offered.

Bobbi waited for Hugh to call her with an update. She waited about an hour and when she didn't hear anything, she tried to read a little. The phone rang and she jumped. She had nodded off a little.

"Hello?"

"Hey Bobbi. It's Hugh honey. I wanted to update you on what's going on with Charlie. We're working on finding out who supplied the drugs to the girls, but still no word about Shirley. We haven't even received any phone calls about or from her. He's worried sick and can't eat or sleep. He's having a bad time of it."

"Of course he is. Poor thing. Is there anything I can do?"

"No, just get better and I will keep you posted. You get out of the hospital tomorrow right?"

"Yes, around noon. I'm going to go down to the office and Mr. Fitzgerald says he has a check for me while I am on rest." Bobbi told him.

"Oh, that's nice of him. It will take away some of the pressure while you take time off."

"Yeah, I wasn't expecting it, but it is a big help. I'm really exhausted Hugh. I'm going to go get some rest. Give my love to Charlie."

"Ok, doll. Talk to you tomorrow."

Bobbi hung up the phone and went to sleep. The stress of everything going on lately had completely wiped her out.

"Why are you keeping me here?" Shirley yelled.
No answer.
"Who are you? Do you know my husband is a detective and the entire police force is looking for me?
Nothing.
Shirley sat down on the bed frustrated. She had tried to eat the sandwich he had left for her earlier, but it tasted funny, and she was willing to bet it was drugged with something. She wasn't feeling well though. It had been hours since she had food or sleep. Maybe she should try to lie down on the bed and rest.
She put her head down, closed her eyes and drifted off to sleep.

Charlie and Hugh went to pick up John Carlton before he tried to skip town. They had some questions for him and wanted to take advantage of the time they had to bring him in while waiting for the drug information.
On the way to pick him up, Charlie broke down. "I don't know what to do, Hugh. I'm sick to death over this. Shirley is my life. I can't help feeling like this is my fault somehow. I'm so lost and don't know what to do to get her back. What if he harms her? I have to find her." He was crying and Hugh just listened.
"You know, I am going to tell you something that I haven't shared with anyone, but you're my best friend, Hugh and I need to get this off my shoulders."
"What is it, Charlie? You have enough to deal with right now, buddy. Why add to it?"
"I haven't been happy lately. This case has been making me doubt my own life. I feel like I have a responsibility to these girls and it's on me to make things

right. I work more than I see my family, and you know what, I would rather work."

Hugh just listened and looked at Charlie.

"I love Shirley with all my heart. We've been together since we were kids, but things haven't been right lately. She knows my heart is more into my work than my marriage. I've hurt her tremendously, Hugh and I have to make it right."

"Charlie, all marriages have ups and downs. That's part of life. You can't blame yourself."

"No, you don't understand. It's more than that. I had an affair."

Hugh didn't know what to say. He had never expected that from Charlie. Many guys cheated on their wives, but he never even considered Charlie to be one who would. His marriage was too strong. Charlie and Shirley were his role models for the perfect marriage.

"It was a brief affair. Just one time with a stranger. But it happened all the same. I had a lot of pressure on myself from the case, things weren't good at home, I met a beautiful woman who had no ties to me, and God help me I made a mistake."

Charlie wasn't going to tell Hugh whom he cheated with, and he hoped Bobbi wouldn't either. What would it solve to tell him? Bobbi and Hugh seemed to be hitting it off really well. They both deserved to be happy. Why cause problems for them over a one-night fling that really meant nothing to either of them?

"It was a one time thing. Nothing even worth discussing. I just feel so damn guilty about it. Now with Shirley missing, I feel like I'm responsible. Like God's punishing me. What other explanation could there be?"

"Oh Charlie. You can't think that way. You'll just drive yourself crazy worrying like that. God's not punishing you. Some sick bastard who gets his rocks off taking women is to blame. It's not your fault."

"Thanks Hugh. I wish I could believe that, but I shouldn't have ever second guessed our marriage. I'm not even worthy of her love to begin with, and now who knows what she's going through?"

"We're doing everything we can, Charlie. Just try to keep your mind on the case. The quicker we follow the clues, the quicker we find her."

The men pulled up to the callbox of John Carlton's house. There were several cars in the driveway but the place felt like a ghost town. Something didn't seem right. They pushed the button on the intercom and Carton's servant answered. "We're here to see your boss. We have a warrant for his arrest," Hugh told her.

"Oh, Mr. Carlton's not here," she said. "He took a vacation with Mrs. Carlton."

"Where did they go?" Charlie asked her.

"To their house in Palm Springs. I can give you the address if you want."

"Yes, please ma'am. We will need it right away," Charlie said.

Hugh and Charlie were quickly on their way to Palm Springs. They couldn't believe that Carlton had taken off when things were going so wrong. He had something to hide, but what? They would have to drive out to Palm Springs, and bring him all the way back for questioning. He wouldn't be happy about that.

A couple of hours later, Hugh and Charlie pulled up to a large gated community. "Can I help you?" The doorman asked. "We need to see Mr. John Carlton," Charlie responded. "We have a warrant for his arrest."

"I'm sorry, but Mr. and Mrs. Carlton aren't here. They went over to the Riviera for the day to get some sun," replied the doorman.

"You've got to be kidding me. We can't seem to track this guy down," Hugh said.

"Well let's head over there. We'll check it out."

They drove up to The Riviera and left the car with the valet. "Don't move it. We won't be long," Hugh told the attendant.

They put their jackets on and walked into the hotel. It was a little chilly out, even for Palm Springs. But, then again, it was only March. As they walked through the resort, they noticed several famous actors and entertainers lounging by the pool. They seemed much more relaxed and less guarded than they did when Charlie ran into them at home. That was understandable. No press here bothering them.

Charlie walked up to one of the waiters. Have you seen a Mr. Carlton today?"

"No, sir, not yet. We've been expecting him though. That's his cabana over there." He pointed to the cabana to the left of the pool.

They walked over to the cabana. It was stocked with liquor, fruit, and ashtrays. They were ready to make some money off of Mr. and Mrs. Carlton. These high class resorts paid attention to the little details to make more money off their clients. Something as simple as chopped fruit could land a huge tip.

Hugh and Charlie decided to take a seat at the bar while they waited for Carlton. "What can I get you gentlemen?" the bartender asked.

"Just coffee for both of us, please," answered Hugh.

Hugh looked at Charlie. He looked like a mere shadow of a man. He had dark circles under his eyes, his hair was disheveled, and he had the same suit on he slept in last night. Hugh felt for him. There was nothing anyone could do right now to make him feel any better. They just had to keep working on the case and hopefully they would find Shirley.

What if they didn't find her though? Hugh thought about the possibility that Shirley could be found like all the other women. If they found Shirley dead like all the others, he feared Charlie would fall apart. With all the pressure and stress he was already experiencing, that would surely send him over the edge. Hugh didn't want to think about that. He prayed they would find her soon.

"Here he comes," Charlie tapped Hugh. "Let's go get him."

They walked over to the cabana just as Carlton and his wife were getting settled. "Gentlemen, what a pleasant surprise. What can I do for you?" Carlton asked smugly. "Honey, what's going on?" Asked Mrs. Carlton.
"Oh nothing, darling, just go grab us both a drink at the bar will you?"
She went toward the bar while the men continued their conversation.

"We're here to take you in, Carlton," Charlie told him.

"What are you talking about, Detective?"

"We need to ask you some questions about the murders we asked you about a couple of days ago. We've had some new developments in the case and think you might be able to help us out," Hugh added.

"As you can see, gentlemen, my wife and I are here celebrating our anniversary. Can't it wait until Monday?"

"I don't think so, Carlton. You see, my wife is missing and I'm going to do whatever it takes to get her back."

"I don't see what that has to do with me, Detective."

"Well, you are connected with Howard Starks who we believe had part in our investigation, and we have an eyewitness who has identified you as one of the men present in the Roosevelt Hotel room, the night one of our victims was found dead."

"I was present at a hotel? You've got to be joking, right?" Carlton asked with an attitude.

"Nope." Charlie told him, defiantly.

"Of course I was at the Roosevelt. I have dinner and drinks there every week. That's all you have?"

"Actually, no," Hugh responded. "We have someone who can place you in the hotel room with the dead woman before she was found. I believe you have a little side business?"

The smile faded from Carlton's face. He looked angry. "What are you referring to?"

"Oh, I think you know. Do we really need to discuss it here? In front of your friends?" Hugh asked. People around the pool were beginning to stare.

"Look, I don't know what you think you have on me, but my wife and I just got here. I'd like to clear this all up on Monday with my attorney."

"Not exactly, Carlton. Charlie's wife is in danger, and this is a little more serious than that. Go tell the Mrs. that you're coming back to town with us."

"Fine. You'll pay for this, I promise you that."

Carlton went over to his wife at the bar, and they appeared to be discussing the situation. She didn't act as though she were surprised. He'd been in trouble before, and she had been through it with him. She kissed him on the cheek and told him she would call their attorney and head back into town.

"Alright, let's go get this over with." He said as they all walked off together.

The drive back to town was long. Charlie couldn't help but feel like it was never ending. He tried to use the time to rest, but couldn't help but try to question Carlton on their way. "Where the hell is my wife, Carlton?"

"I have no idea what you're talking about, Detective, and I resent your tone."

"You know what, cut the shit. You know exactly what I'm talking about, and don't think for a second I won't pull this car over and beat it out of you."

Hugh couldn't believe he was harassing the suspect before they even made it back to town. It was completely against policy to question anyone without their attorney present. He needed to get Charlie to calm down long enough to take a nap and cool off. "Hey Charlie, lay back and rest, man. Let me take care of this when we get back."

"Yeah, listen to your partner, Charlie. You don't want a lawsuit for threatening me," Carlton responded.

It took everything he had in him to ignore this prick. *Calm down*, Charlie, he told himself. *Don't lose it now. You need to stay calm to find Shirley.* Charlie leaned back, closed his eyes and fell asleep.

When he woke, they were back at the station. "Hey buddy, we're here," Hugh said.

Charlie felt sick again. Every time he slept, waking up was painful. He wanted this whole thing to be over.

They went into the station, placed Carlton in a room, and went for some coffee.

"I think we should both question him," Hugh suggested.

"Fine, but none of this bad cop, good cop crap. We need to lay into him. We're wasting time, Hugh."

Just as they were about to take a break, Charlie received a call from his mother.

"Charlie, the kids are wondering when you're coming home. They miss their mother, and are starting to ask a lot of questions. I think some of their friends at school have been saying things." She told him.

"I'm so sorry Mom to have to put you in this position. I don't know what to tell them. What do you think?" He asked her.

"I don't know, sweetie. They're your children. You have to decide what's best for them. I'm sure whatever you decide will be the right choice."

"I just can't make these decisions without Shirley. I don't even know what to say to them. I will try to make it home a little early today to spend some time with them. I'll see if I can straighten things out."

Charlie hung up the phone. He had so much on his mind. He didn't even know where to begin. He was so close to having a complete breakdown. The only things keeping him going was the kids, and of course his need to find Shirley.

They headed back into the interrogation room to question Carlton. He knew more than he was telling and Charlie vowed he would beat it out of him if that's what it took. This piece of shit held the clues to find Shirley and he would stop at nothing to find her.

"Where is she!" Charlie yelled.

"Whom are you referring to?" Carlton responded. He was taunting them.

"Look, Carlton. I know you're involved in this and I will bring you down. If anything happens to my wife, you will be sorry."

"I refuse to speak to you gentlemen until my attorney is present," Carlton responded.

"Of course. We'll leave you to wait for him then," said Hugh.

They walked out into the office and decided what their next step should be. "Buddy, you cannot go at this guy in a way that will piss him off," Hugh told Charlie. "We have to really try to get to him so he's backed into a corner and we can move on to the next clue."

"I'm trying, Hugh, but how would you feel if it were your wife missing and the piece of shit responsible for it was in the next room, refusing to talk?"

"I'm so sorry for all you're going through, Charlie, but if you don't hold it together, the Captain will remove you from the case. You're too close. You need to be objective."

"You're right. Maybe you and O'Malley should question him. I need to get some air. I'm taking a walk. I'll be back in an hour."

Chapter 22

Bobbi was feeling much better about things this morning. She was released from the hospital and was on her way to pick up the check that Mr. Fitzgerald had offered her. She still couldn't believe his generosity. Maybe she had been wrong about him all these years, assuming he was only out to take care of himself. He had been involved in some horrible things, as she saw in the files, but everyone made mistakes, and who was she to judge?

She was excited to be outside. The weather was nice. Not too cold, but a little brisk. She thought she would stop on the way to get a quick cup of coffee at the coffee shop. Just as she was about to walk in, she saw Charlie sitting on the bench outside. "Charlie?"

He looked up. He looked exhausted. "Hi Bobbi. How are you feeling?"

"I'm fine. But, how are you feeling? You look awful."

"Thanks a lot."

"I'm sorry Charlie. I didn't mean that."

"Oh, I know, Bobbi. I'm sorry, I'm tired and cranky. Just ignore me. I have a lot on my mind."

"I bet. Hugh has been updating me with what's been happening. I'm so sorry Charlie. Is there anything I can do?"

"No, thanks though, Bobbi. We're working on it. I appreciate everything you've done so far. How are things with you and Hugh?"

"Good, so far. I wanted to talk to you about that." She said.

"No need to say anything, Bobbi. I wasn't even going to mention us to him at all. There's no reason to. He seems really happy with you, and what we had was a mistake for both of us."

Bobbi felt a huge sense of relief. She had been worried that Charlie would share their relationship with Hugh, and Hugh wouldn't want to pursue anything with her. Now she didn't need to worry about that.

Although Bobbi did have feelings for Charlie, she knew getting involved with him was a mistake from the beginning. They had a fling. Nothing serious, and nothing to jeopardize long term happiness over. She was done with picking the wrong guys. "Oh, good, I'm glad you feel the same way, Charlie. I really like Hugh and want to see where things go. He's such a sweetheart and I think we would be good together."

"I do too. I hope things work out for you two."

"Well, I don't want to cut you short, Bobbi, but I have to get back to the station. Anything you want me to pass along to Hugh?"

"Oh, if you would. Could you tell him that I'm going to pick up a check from my boss and should be home after that if he wants to stop by or call."

"Will do. Take care Bobbi."

"You too, Charlie."

Bobbi felt such relief when she entered the coffee shop. It seemed like things were really beginning to get better for her. *Poor Charlie*, she thought. *I wish there was something I could do for him.* Bobbi paid for her coffee and headed on to the office.

Bobbi walked into the office about 3:30. There weren't too many people around. In fact, the place seemed a little like a ghost town. Well, it was a Friday. Many of the attorneys left early on Fridays, and allowed their secretaries to do the same. Still, it felt a little quiet.

"Hey Bobbi. How are you feeling honey?" One of the secretaries, Elizabeth asked.

"I'm feeling a lot better thanks for asking. I'm just stopping in to see Mr. Fitzgerald for a bit."

"Oh, I think I saw him head out for a quick cigarette. His temp left for the day, so just go wait in his office for him."

"Oh thanks Liz. I'll see you next week," Bobbi told her.

Bobbi looked around her desk to see if there was anything pressing she needed to be aware of. Everything looked pretty normal. Nothing to worry about. *The temp seems to be keeping up on things*, she thought. It felt strange being here as a visitor, rather than an employee. The office was like her second home for such a large part of her life, and she had decided over this last week that she didn't want to be here forever. She wanted more for her life than to be someone's secretary. Everything she had gone through had changed her perspective on life completely.

Being independent didn't mean you had to completely give up being a wife and mother. She understood now how her mother had catered to her father all these years. They were in love. When you were in love you did things for each other. You were selfless. Maybe Bobbi hadn't ever truly been in love. She only watched out for herself. Since seeing what Charlie was going through, and meeting Hugh, she felt different.

Maybe Hugh was the one for her, maybe he wasn't, but she wanted to try. She wanted to live for someone else beside herself for a change. She wanted the husband, kids, and stable family life. She was a little shocked that she had gone through such a drastic change in thinking. But, traumatizing events often had a way of doing that to you. She didn't want to waste another day living just for herself.

Bobbi was smiling at her newfound maturity, when Mr. Fitzgerald walked in. "Oh, hello Bobbi. How are you feeling darling?" He looked really thin and a little stressed.

"Much better, thanks, sir. I just need some time to get things in order. After everything going on, I'm a little behind."

"Well, that's completely understandable. The doctor who called in for you didn't really share much with me. Are you ok?" He asked.

"Yes, I'd just rather not talk about it if that's ok with you, sir. It's kind of a private matter."

"Oh, of course. I just thought the police were involved somehow, because some detectives called to ask me some questions about you."

"About me? Do you know which detectives they were?"

"I believe a Detective Fenton. But it was right before you went into the hospital."

Bobbi was relieved. She thought for a second that Hugh had been checking up on her for some reason, but realized he was getting information before they met.

"Well, anyway, sir. I hate to rush you, but I have to get down to the store before five. I'm having a small dinner and need to get some last minute things." She moved toward his office.

"Sure, stay here and relax, just let me get the check. I'll be right back."

He walked into his office. Bobbi sat back down and waited for him while she thought of Hugh. She couldn't wait until all of this was over so they could spend some time getting to know each other. She was so lost in her thoughts that she didn't even see Mr. Fitzgerald come back out with the gun.

"Bobbi I need you to come with me," he said.

She looked up and realized he had a gun pointed at her. She was shocked. "Mr. Fitzgerald what are you doing?"

"You know damn well what I'm doing. You know I was involved in that little group of men with the missing women, and I'm not going to jail. I'm taking you with me for a bit while I decide what to do."

"Mr. Fitzgerald, this is crazy. You're not involved enough for anyone to even care about you." She said as she started backing away from his office. "I saw your pictures, yes, but that's it. I never mentioned your name to anyone, and I don't even think they knew you were involved at all."

"Well, too bad for you, honey I can't take that chance. I will not have this ruin me." He held the gun so shakily that she thought it might go off by mistake.

"So what, you're going to kidnap me? What the hell are you thinking? You are ruining your life on your own!"

"Be quiet! I need time to think. You're going to come with me for a little drive, while I figure this all out."

Fitzgerald walked Bobbi through the lobby after telling her not to make a motion or a sound. He had the gun pressed into her side under his coat. As they were leaving, people barely glanced at them, not noticing anything was amiss. Bobbi tried to make eye contact with any of the employees, but no one seemed to notice her. One of them even said, "Goodnight, Miss Brooks, Mr. Fitzgerald." Bobbi knew once they exited the building she was in some real trouble.

"Where do you think you're going?" She asked him. "You won't get away with this. I'm having dinner with one of the detectives tonight, and he will come looking for me when I stand him up."

"We'll see about that sweetheart." He pushed her into his car and they took off down the block.

Chapter 23

John Carlton finally started talking a little once his attorney arrived. He didn't say much, but gave the detectives enough information for them to start new leads. According to Carlton, he was second in charge of the prostitution business for about three years. His boss was a man named Joseph Gambini. He didn't have much contact with Gambini. Carlton basically ran the business and just passed the books on to him.

Carlton also went on to say that he knew nothing of Shirley's disappearance. He helped to cover up one bad situation for a client of theirs, named Sam, but that's all the contact he had had with him. Carlton knew Sam as a quiet guy who didn't come around much, and when he did, he was in, out, and on his way. Carton didn't like dealing with him because he was so picky. He never got the man's last name and tried not to ask too many questions. He wanted to know little, if anything about his clients.

Hugh didn't know why, but he believed Carlton, and didn't believe he had anything to do with Shirley's disappearance.

"Are we done here, Detective?" Carlton's attorney asked.

"Yeah, we're done. For now," Hugh answered. "Don't go anywhere in case we need to talk with you again."

Hugh and O'Malley came out of the interrogation room.

"How'd it go?" Charlie asked.

"Well, he didn't know much, but we did get some information on his boss, a Joseph Gambini. I thought you and I could take a ride out to talk with him. He lives in Beverly Hills."

"Nothing more than that?" Charlie asked, amazed.

"No, sorry man. We're doing everything we can. I believe Carlton. He doesn't seem to be hiding anything."

"Ok, let's get some coffee and get going."

"Oh, you know what? I have to call Bobbi first to tell her I will be a little late. We're having dinner tonight."

"Things are going good with you two then?" Charlie asked.

"Yeah, I really like her. It'll be nice to spend some time with her tonight, just the two of us."

"Ok, go call her and I'll meet you in the car."

Charlie walked out to the car and felt sick all over again. He couldn't focus on anything, it seemed, and every minute that passed he feared a greater chance of losing Shirley. Obviously the person who took her didn't want money or to get back at him in some way, or they would have heard from him by now. This scared Charlie even more. That meant other motives. Charlie wouldn't allow himself to think about that. He had to stay focused and positive for her and the kids.

Hugh came walking out to the car with a look of confusion on his face.

"What's wrong?" Charlie asked him.

"Oh, it's probably nothing, but Bobbi was supposed to be home making dinner and there was no answer. We were supposed to eat at six so she said she'd be cooking from about four o'clock on."

"She probably just ran to the store or something," Charlie said.

"Yeah, you're probably right. I just get worried with everything going on, I guess. Well, let's get going. See what we can find out from this Gambini."

Shirley tried to scream as loud as she could. Nothing. No one was around to hear her. That meant she was probably out in the middle of nowhere. How was anyone going to find her? She still hadn't had contact from her captor, other than to give her some food.

The door opened. A fairly large man with a surgeon's mask entered the room. He was walking toward Shirley. What could she do? He was holding some type of needle. Shirley tried to kick him and run, but he was too strong for her. He stopped her, and held her arm while he injected something into it. Shirley felt herself getting very sleepy. She completely lost all strength and fell to the floor.

"Well you are a fighter," he said, before he closed the door again.

Charlie and Hugh pulled up to the gate of Gambini's house. House might not be the right word. Mansion was more like it. Charlie pressed the button on the intercom. A voice answered. "Yes?"

"Detectives Brower and Fenton from LAPD homicide division. We need to speak to Mr. Gambini." Charlie answered.

"Just a moment please," the voice responded.

A few moments later, the gates opened. "I guess we pull up the drive, huh?" Charlie asked Hugh.

"It looks like someone is out front waiting for us."

They pulled up and got out. "Detectives, please follow me," the woman, who appeared to be a servant requested.

As they walked in the house, it was hard not to notice the grandeur of it all. The house was absolutely gorgeous and a little breathtaking. "Wow," Hugh said under his breath. "What kind of business do you think he's in? He joked.

"Have a seat Detectives. Mr. Gambini will be right with you."

"Can't wait to hear what this prick has to say," Charlie said.

"Charlie, you need to calm down. We can't piss him off right off the bat. We need to get some information from him. You need to be patient."

"Alright, Hugh. It's your show. I'll just listen."

A man came through the foyer and looked very surprised to see the detectives. "What can I do for you gentlemen? I'm Joe Gambini."

"Mr. Gambini, I'm Detective Hugh Fenton, and this is my partner, Detective Charles Brower. We're investigating the Hollywood murder case, you might have heard of it?"

"Is that the case where the young girls are being found on the streets? What a shame. A damn shame."

"Yes, it is. We are trying to solve the case and put the miserable killer behind bars, but we need some help." Hugh told the man.

"I don't know how I could possibly help you gentlemen, but I'll try."

"Do you know a Howard Starks?" Hugh asked.

"No. Should I?"

"Not necessarily. How about a James Carlton?"

"Yes, I know James. He works for me. Is he in some kind of trouble?"

"Not exactly. What type of work does Mr. Carlton do for you?"

"Look, fella's, if you're here asking about him, you obviously know what business I'm in. Can we cut the shit and get to the point here? I have a tennis game to play." Gambini said as he poured himself a drink.

"Alright. Bottom line here is we have several missing girls and we're trying to prevent any more from going missing. We have one missing right now and we need your help to point us to any contacts you might have," Charlie said.

"I'd love to help you out, but I have no idea who would want to hurt those girls. I think what they're doing is sick."

"We're looking for a man who we only know as Sam. Anyone stand out for you that might have ordered prostitutes and acted a little strangely around them?"

"Most guys who order prostitutes in that way are a little strange to begin with. I can't think of anything out of the ordinary. There was a guy named Sam who called for the service quite frequently, but I don't know much about him. Carlton would be the one to ask. He has more contact with the customers than I do." Gambini told them.

"Well, here's my card," Hugh told him. "If you do think of anything, can you please give us a call? I don't want to get involved in your business. We just need your help."

"I will. Like I said, I don't condone what this sick son of a bitch is doing. Women are precious. The fact that he is killing some of the best looking in the area, especially some who have worked for me doesn't sit well with me. I'll be looking for him, don't you worry."

"Just don't do anything stupid if you do find him," Hugh said. "We need to ask him some questions about the missing girl while he's still coherent."

"Sure detective, I'll let you question him first. Then we'll take care of him after."

The men walked down the driveway toward the car. "Thanks for your time," Charlie called after him.

"No problem. Good luck."

On the way back to the station, Hugh voiced his concerns over this missing "Sam."

"Charlie, it's like the guy is a ghost. No one seems to know who he is. How are we supposed to find him if everyone in his immediate circle can't even give us his name?"

"I'm not sure. I just know that we have half the crooks in town looking for him too. He'll turn up soon, I'm sure of it."

Hugh asked Charlie if he minded if they stopped at Bobbi's place on their way back. "No problem, I'll just wait in the car." Charlie said.

Hugh walked up the steps to Bobbi's apartment. It looked dark inside. There was no answer and no smell of cooking coming from the building. That's really odd, Hugh thought. Where was she? They were supposed to be meeting for dinner in an hour. Hugh walked back to the car with a sour look on his face.

"What's wrong now?"

"She's still not home and the apartment is dark." Hugh said with a frown.

"Well, maybe she hasn't been home yet. I'm sure she's fine."

"Maybe. But I have a bad feeling."

Chapter 24

"You're crazy! Where do you think you're going to take me?" Bobbi screamed.

"Bobbi, shut the hell up, you crazy bitch! I need to think." Fitzgerald waved the gun at her.

He was driving around in circles. He seemed unsure of his plan. He hadn't thought this through at all, obviously. Because of this, Bobbi thought she had a chance to escape. She was sitting in the front seat of the car. He had the gun on her. She could either open the door and fall out, taking her chances, or she could kick the steering wheel, taking the chance of killing them both.

He seemed to be taking her out to some remote area in the Angeles National Forest. She knew if he got her to wherever they were going, she wouldn't come out alive. But, she had to try to stay in the car as long as possible to help Charlie find the others, and possibly his wife. *Stay calm Bobbi.* She told herself. *He's a huge part of these murders and he will never let me get away alive. I've got to do something fast.*

They made a quick turn and Bobbi took her chance. She opened the car door, jumped out, and began rolling down the hill. When she came to the bottom she felt like she hit her head on something hard. She struggled to get up, and with all the energy she had, she turned around and ran in the opposite direction.

She needed to get to the highway so someone could give her a ride before Fitzgerald found her. She was exhausted and could barely walk, but she had to continue on.

Concentrate, Bobbi, she told herself. *You have to get out of here to help the others.* A man pulled up to her as she was climbing the embankment. He stopped the truck, got out and ran over to her.

"Are you ok Miss?" He asked her.

"I'm alright, but I need a ride back to town right away please."

He helped her into the truck and they were on their way back toward Hollywood. She asked the man to take her to the police station so she could tell Charlie and Hugh what had happened.

Hugh couldn't concentrate. Where is she? He wondered. With everything going on, maybe he was overreacting, but he had an unsettling feeling in his stomach. Bobbi had been really excited about their date, so he knew she wouldn't have stood him up. It just didn't make sense.

Just as he was about to call her for the twentieth time, the desk sergeant on duty told him there was someone there to see him.

Hugh walked up to the front of the station, and gasped. "Oh my God, Bobbi, honey, what happened to you?" He ran to help hold her up before she passed out.

"I need to sit down, Hugh and I will tell you everything I can."

He ushered her into the station, called for someone to bring the first aid kit, and sat her down in a chair at his desk. "What happened to you, sweetheart? I've been worried sick. I think you need to go to the hospital. Your head is bleeding."

Bobbi was filthy, had dried blood on her head and face, and her hair and makeup were a huge mess. She had also clearly been crying, as mascara was streaming down her face.

"I do need to go to the hospital, Hugh. I think I might have a concussion, but I need to tell you and Charlie what happened. It might help him find Shirley."

"Stay here, baby, I'll go get him. Just rest ok?"

Hugh ran off to find Charlie while Bobbi put her head in her hands. One of the other detectives was using the first aid kit to clean her up a little. "Do you need to use the facilities or anything, ma'am?" He asked.

"No, thank you so much. I'm fine. Maybe just a drink of water?"

He grabbed her the water and she drank just as Hugh and Charlie came running back over to her.

"Oh my God, Bobbi, what the hell happened to you?" Charlie asked.

"Just a little accident is all. I'm fine, but I have some information for you."

She drank another sip of the water and continued. "Fitzgerald is in on these murders. I don't know exactly how, but he is involved. He held me at gunpoint and forced me into his car. I went there to pick up a check and he had other plans."

"Your boss? The attorney?" Charlie asked her.

"Yes. He had some pictures in his file that showed him and some other women in compromising positions a few weeks ago when this whole thing started. I assumed he was into ordering hookers, nothing more. I thought he was a creep for it, but not a murderer. I had no idea that he knew I saw the photos, but he must have."

"Did you recognize any of the girls in the photos?" Hugh asked.

"I'm not sure. I saw the photos before I ever met any of the girls in the hotel. I would need to see them again."

"We need to get those photos now Hugh, so we can identify any of the dead girls to give Fitzgerald motive and tie him to these murders," Charlie said.

"I'll call the judge right now to issue a search warrant." Hugh told them as he went to his desk to make the call.

While Hugh was on the phone, Charlie asked Bobbi what else happened.

"Well, he decided he didn't know what his next step would be, so he was going to take me with him for a while, until he could figure it out. We rode in the car for what seemed like at least an hour. He was acting really erratic. He wasn't making much sense, but he wasn't really telling me anything either. He just said he didn't know what to do yet, and until he figured it out, I was going for a ride with him."

Hugh hung up the phone. "We're waiting for the warrant now. They're working on it. What happened next honey?"

"We started making our way out to the Angeles National Forest and I had a really bad feeling I would never come out if I went in. I started to wonder if I should kick the steering wheel, but decided to open the door and jump out. When I did, I rolled down the hill and he took off."

"The Angeles National Forest?" Charlie asked.

"Yes, I thought you might want to check somewhere in that area for Shirley or any other girls who are missing."

"Bobbi, you are extremely brave. I can't thank you enough for trying to hold on to get information that could help us find Shirley," Charlie said, and he kissed her on the cheek.

"I'm going to head out to Fitzgerald's office to see what I can find. Why don't you take Bobbi to the hospital and we will head out to the forest when the warrant is good."

"Alright, partner. Keep in touch."

Bobbi and Hugh left for the hospital, while Charlie planned out his route for the forest. He had no intention of waiting for Hugh. He knew that Shirley was up there somewhere and he'd be damned if he waited for some piece of paper to find his wife. Charlie put on his jacket and headed out toward his car.

Shirley woke up feeling really sick. "What the hell did you give me?" She shouted. The door opened and the man with the mask came in again. This time, though, he carried her out toward another dark room. The room had a long table with bright lights above it. It appeared to be some type of operating table. "Where am I?" She asked.

"Don't worry about it darling. Everything will be explained soon enough." He responded.

The sound of his voice in her ear made her ill. She couldn't feel her legs. She had no control of her body at all. She knew what was going on around her, but it was very cloudy. There was another man in the room. She couldn't see him very well. He had a suit and hat on. He appeared to be sitting in the dark, just watching her.

"Are you ready?" The man in the mask asked the other.

"Yes, we've delayed on this one long enough." The other man said.

"Alright, turn on the radio. It's time for some fun."

The last thing Shirley saw was a man coming at her with a huge scalpel.

Chapter 25

Charlie was on his way up the mountain and couldn't stop thinking about his wife. She had always been so loving. How could he have ever cheated on her? All she ever did was love him. He chose his job over her and the kids time and time again, yet he was the one to stray. He was supposed to protect her, how could he let this happen to her? He began to feel sick, but kept on up the highway.

Charlie reached the area of the mountain that Bobbi described. He got out of the car and looked around. Just as he did a car came flying around the mountain and almost hit him. "Hey! Watch where the hell you're goin!" He yelled after the car.

He didn't see much there, so he decided to get back into the car and drive on further. He was letting both his heart and his detective intuition guide him. As he approached the next corner, he found a small shack and stopped. Strange, he thought aloud. How could someone live all the way up here? It had to be an old miners cabin or something.

He got out of the car and began to wander around. The first thing he smelled when he walked on a little further was the familiar scent of decay. He pulled his gun and went on alert. This had to be the place, he thought. He looked around carefully, but didn't see anyone. After securing the scene, he continued to look around for bodies. "Shirley?" He called. No answer. Just stillness. It was too calm. He couldn't find Shirley or anyone else around the deserted shack. Charlie began to look around the dilapidated building. He entered the front door, and walked into what looked like the main room. The smell overtook him. He had to run outside and vomit. When he returned to the scene he had his kerchief covering his mouth and nose. He knew one or more bodies were somewhere on the premises.

As Charlie continued through the small house, he found blood spots on the floor of what appeared to be a makeshift kitchen. He bent down to examine them and they were fresh. Someone had just been here. He continued on through the house. It was extremely dark and musty. He came to a room that had a huge operating table with large, overhead lights. *What the hell?*

He continued to examine the table and the equipment around it. Someone paid a small fortune for all this equipment just to abandon it. Charlie started to panic. It looked like some type of modern torture device. There were tools all around the table, some with blood still on them. He started praying that Shirley was not anywhere near this mess.

Before he went any further, Charlie ran out to the car, and radioed for backup. He needed someone to come out to the shack and investigate. He didn't want to think about digging up bodies. The thought of those poor girls buried somewhere near made his stomach turn.

"Dispatch, this is Detective Charlie Brower. I need immediate crime scene investigators up in the Angeles National Forest."

"Roger that Brower. They're on their way," dispatch responded.

Charlie waited around for the team to get there. He had a sinking feeling that Shirley had been here. He didn't want to watch them dig, but felt like he had no choice. He had to find out what happened here for his own peace of mind.

At the hospital, Hugh tried to call the station looking for Charlie. There was no answer. *Where the hell is he?* Hugh thought. *I hope he didn't head out there on his own or do anything stupid.* He tried the station again.

The desk sergeant told Hugh he saw Charlie run out about an hour ago, and he had recently called for backup. "Damn it! I knew he would do this." Hugh said as he slammed down the telephone.

"Bobbi, honey are you ok by yourself?" Hugh asked her.

"Of course, why?" She asked.

"Charlie decided to take off to the forest by himself and I have to head up there. Who knows what he'll find. We don't even have the warrant yet. He could get suspended over something stupid like this, and worse ruin our chances of a conviction."

"I'll be fine, just hurry. Get to him in case he finds something he can't handle. We'll meet up later." She responded.

"I'm so glad you're ok baby. I will be in touch." Hugh kissed her and left the hospital.

On the way back to the station, Hugh radioed dispatch to confirm there were backup units on their way to the Angeles National Forest. He turned the car around and headed up to the forest area. Poor Charlie, he thought. I hope he didn't find Shirley there.

Charlie stood outside waiting for the bodies to be unearthed. Most of the victims had been left in the city, but with the horrible stench up here, it was clear there were more they were unaware of.

"We got one," the coroner called.

Charlie held his breath. He prayed it wasn't Shirley.

"Dark haired female. Looks fairly fresh. Rigormortis just setting in. Looks to be only a few hours old."

Charlie forced himself to look. He only saw the left hand and the wedding ring on it, before he turned around and fainted. When he came too, the coroner was sitting with him trying to revive him. "Charlie, I'm so sorry." He said.

Charlie felt like he were having a nightmare. This couldn't be true. His wife had been alive just a few days ago, smiling, laughing, and playing with their children. Now, she was dead and buried in a makeshift grave. How could he ever go on with his life? What would he tell the kids? How could he ever do his job well again? He couldn't even save his own wife. Charlie couldn't focus on what was happening around him. He felt that the life he knew was over in a matter of minutes. He just sat with his head down and prayed for some strength.

Hugh arrived at the scene some time later. The mood was somber as all murder scenes were, but this one felt particularly morose. He knew something wasn't right, and prayed it wasn't Shirley.

As soon as he walked up the embankment to the shack and saw Charlie, he knew. *Oh my God,* he thought. *Not Shirley.*

"Charlie?" Hugh called.

Charlie looked up but didn't say a word. He just burst into tears and began uncontrollably sobbing. In all the years they had been partners, Hugh had never seen Charlie break down. Although it was nice to know he wasn't made of stone, Hugh couldn't bear to see the pain he was in.

Hugh went over to him and the two embraced. Charlie wouldn't let go and felt like he could collapse at any moment. "Oh, buddy. I'm so sorry." Hugh told him. "What can I do?"

Charlie just shook his head and sat down. Hugh went over to the paramedics and told them to take Charlie to the hospital so he could be checked out for possible shock.

"Come on buddy. We're going to take a little ride down to the hospital to get you checked out." Hugh escorted Charlie to the ambulance.

As soon as they left, Hugh began walking the scene. "What do we have, guys?"

"It's bad, Hugh. This place looks like a cemetery. So many dead bodies, and the condition they're in is sickening. Charlie's wife is one of the worst." One of the medics told him.

Hugh couldn't bear to look at her, but had to in order to get a sense of what they were getting themselves into. Poor thing. She looked like she had been tortured and beaten down. There were cigarette marks all over her body, especially on her breast area. She was cut open from breast to stomach, and had been stitched up again. Her ears were bleeding, toenails ripped off, and of course, one of her teeth were missing. "Jesus." Hugh said. "I will kill this son of a bitch when I find him."

They continued to process the scene. It took hours and hours to get all the bodies up. In all, there were eighteen. This was the worst serial killer case Los Angeles had ever seen. How on earth were they going to process all these bodies? Hopefully someone could identify these girls so they could avoid being just more Jane Doe's.

Hugh drove back to the station, lost in his thoughts. He tried to separate his job from his personal life, but how could one not let what he'd seen affect him and his outlook on people? Not only did he just help process eighteen bodies, but one of them was his best friend's wife! He wanted to quit. He couldn't imagine doing another day of this. He had never felt this way before. No matter how bad things got, he always loved his job. Today, he wanted nothing to do with being a cop. He drove straight to the hospital to check up on both Bobbi and Charlie.

Chapter 26

Hugh left the hospital that night and began to look into Fitzgerald's background. He had to learn as much as he could about the man in order to understand how to catch him. James Fitzgerald was an only child who grew up in Pensacola, Florida.

His early childhood was nothing out of the norm, except that he got into some trouble with the law for trying to hurt animals. He went through some counseling and the authorities thought he was fine to be released.

In high school, he had a few girlfriends, but seemed unable to perform when they tried to make love. He was made fun of because of this, and began to despise women. He felt terribly inadequate and insecure. He was often the outcast of his friends, so he spent a lot of his time at home alone.

After high school, he decided to join the army, but went AWOL after just a few months. He couldn't take the pressure and responsibilities of being in the service. His insecurity only increased in the army, when the drill sergeants made him feel like he was nothing.

He hitched rides to get to California, where he heard there were plenty of girls, drugs, and opportunities. He enrolled at UCLA and began working on his English degree. He decided to become an attorney and enrolled in law school, while he worked at a local deli. He studied hard, but didn't have much of a life outside of school and work.

One day, while he was working at the deli, a beautiful blonde came in alone. She was sitting by herself waiting for someone, and he decided to give it a shot.

"Can I get you something darling?" He asked her.

"No, not yet. I'm just waiting for my boyfriend," she said.

"Ok, you let me know, but if you were my girlfriend, I would never make you wait around for me." He told her and went back to work.

That's all it took, and Judy was smitten with James from then on.

They married in June, and had their first child the following year. James was starting to do well in his firm and there was talk of him becoming partner. He seemed to be on the fast track.

There were no arrests, no trouble, nothing out of the ordinary. Fitzgerald had everything going for him. Until, he asked his wife to let him slap her around a little during their lovemaking. She had been so revolted by the request that they hadn't been intimate in months. Fitzgerald couldn't take it anymore. He needed his wife. He decided to punish her by seeking out other women.

He headed down to some of the seediest areas in Hollywood and cruised around looking for prostitutes. There was nothing of interest to him there, so he decided to try again the next night. In the meantime, he thought he would go eat in Chinatown. It was there he met Sam and his beautiful China girls.

From then on, the girls were like a drug to Fitzgerald. He couldn't get enough. They were all he thought about. Every thought he had revolved around the girls. He became obsessed. He continued to see them until it wasn't enough any more. That's when he became involved in Sam's operation.

Wow, Hugh thought, after reading his file. Hugh knew that Fitzgerald was just a pawn in Sam's game, but still a very disturbed man, just the same. Hugh had to get to Fitzgerald before he made a bad situation worse.

Chapter 27

Two men pulled into a gas station in Phoenix, Arizona. They were arguing and looked like they might get into a fist fight. "God damn it Sam! You messed up the whole fucking plan! They're coming after us now for sure." Fitzgerald screamed.

"Me? I'm not the one who kidnapped his secretary." Sam replied.

"I had to take her with us. I had no plans of letting her escape. Now she will ruin us for sure. Why the hell did you have to kill the cop's wife? We were supposed to let her go as a warning to them."

"You don't make the rules here Fitz. I do. Don't you forget who's in charge. I would hate to take care of this little operation by myself."

They walked into the gas station and bought some cigarettes and two cups of coffee. They were on their way to Texas, where Fitz had a vacation home. They could pick up right where they left off in Texas. The girls in Hollywood were so much prettier, but they couldn't take the chance of returning there for a while. Inside the station, was a pretty young thing asking the attendant for some help. "Excuse me sir? I know you just filled up my tank, but can I get you to check my tire pressure also? I'm on my way to visit my fiancée and don't want anything to slow me down." Sam overheard her.

Sam looked at Fitz, who looked like the cat that swallowed the canary and the men slowly returned to their car. They waited for her to come out, get her air, and drive off. They followed her at a slow pace, so she wouldn't notice anything peculiar. At the next stoplight, Fitz ran out of the car and pulled the woman out of her vehicle. She screamed and kicked, but he overpowered her. They left her car sitting in the middle of the road and drove off with the young woman before anyone saw anything.

At the hospital, Bobbi was doing much better. Charlie, on the other hand had to be sedated because he wouldn't calm down. Understandable, after all he had been going through. Hugh called Charlie's mother from the hospital room and told her everything. She sobbed. Charlie's father had to pick up the phone and said they would be down with the kids immediately.

While Charlie slept, Hugh went to check Bobbi out. "I'm so sorry, Hugh." Bobbi said. "Charlie must be devastated. What can we do to help him get through this?"

"I'm not sure, honey. I've never seen him like this. He's usually a rock. His parents are on their way down with the kids. It breaks my heart to think of him having to tell the kids that their mommy is dead."

"What can you do to continue the investigation and find Fitzgerald?"

"Well we have an APB out for him right now. Hopefully he's still in his car and hasn't lifted someone else's. We will be able to track him down faster that way. The only delay will be if he's crossed into another state. It's hard to get help from out of state police. It takes more time."

"You have to find him, Hugh. He is one sick son of a bitch and will continue trying to hurt women. I know he's involved in these murders. If you don't find him quickly, he will strike again."

Charlie's parents came down to the hospital and stayed with him. They needed to call the funeral home to make the arrangements. As painful as it was for them, Charlie was no where ready to take care of them on his own. He was being fed through a tube, and was probably going to have to spend a few days in the hospital to be treated for shock.

The funeral was going to be on Saturday, three days from now. They hoped Charlie would be well enough by then to attend. All of the detectives and police force came to visit Charlie in the hospital. They couldn't imagine what he had been going through.

The kids were doing ok, but needed their father. Charlie had given up on life and they didn't know if he would ever be the same again.

Fitzgerald and Sam disposed of the girls' body, like all the rest, by burying her. They had begun living in Fitzgerald's vacation home in Dallas, Texas and were at it again. It was great not to be recognized. They had so much freedom here. The possibilities were endless.

It had been two weeks and there was still no sign of any police. It seemed impossible that they would be caught. Fitzgerald had called his wife fairly quickly after they disappeared and she was mortified. She had told him the police had been to their house and were questioning her. All of their friends and family were shocked and embarrassed at the possibility of him being a murderer. He assured her he was not involved, but simply had to take off for a while until things cooled down. She seemed to believe him.

Fitzgerald was getting a little sick of Sam telling him what to do. He wanted the man dead, but hadn't figured out how to do it yet. Every time they picked up a woman, Sam had to make all the decisions. He had to decide who got to touch her, when, how she would die, basically he dictated all the fun. It wasn't fair. Fitzgerald was just as much a part of this as he was. Why did he think he could order him around? Fitzgerald wondered.

Bobbi and Hugh had tried to take care of Charlie for the past few weeks. They had brought him meals, taken the children out to play, and just kept him company. He was a

mess. Hugh wasn't sure if he would ever recover from this.
He hadn't even talked about going back to work. Hugh had
been working on the case with another detective in the
department while Charlie was on leave.

Hugh had worked day and night on the case, but
had no new leads. It was as if Fitzgerald and this other
man, "Sam" had virtually disappeared. He had called
police departments across the state, even into Nevada, but
no one had seen the men. The only thing left to do was
wait. At least the murders in the area had stopped, but
Hugh knew it was only a matter of time before they began
again somewhere else.

The relationship between Bobbi and Hugh was
going really well. The tragic events surrounding Shirley's
death had actually brought them closer. They were
exclusively dating and had even talked about marriage.
Bobbi had never felt so close to a man before. He was
everything she needed and more. Hugh was kind, patient,
loving, and sincere. He made her feel special every day.
She couldn't ever remember being so happy.

Hugh felt the same way about Bobbi. He had
introduced her to his family over dinner one night, and they
all loved her. Bobbi was beautiful, affectionate, and a real
sweetheart. They did everything together and he had
thought about marrying her.

At dinner one night, they ran into Joe Gambini.
"Ah, Detective Fenton. How are you sir?" He asked.

"Mr. Gambini, nice to see you. This is my
girlfriend Bobbi Brooks."

"Nice to meet you darling. Aren't you a beauty."
He shook her hand.

"Thank you. Nice to meet you too," she said.

"How is the case going? Any new developments?"
He asked Hugh.

"Actually quite a bit, but we're stalled for now. Did you hear about Detective Brower's wife?"

"I did, and I was very sorry to learn that bit of bad news. I told you I don't support this behavior, and will do anything I can to help catch Mrs. Brower's killer. Please let me know what I can do." He began to walk away, and stopped. "Oh, by the way, did you know that Fitzgerald has a vacation house in Texas? Just thought you might want to know." With that, he turned and walked off.

"Why would he tell you that?" Bobbi asked Hugh.

"Because he thinks Fitzgerald is a piece of shit and wants to help us catch him."

"You better drop me off and get to the station honey."

"Thanks Bobbi. How did I get so lucky?"

"I don't know, but you did." She laughed.

Chapter 28

Hugh picked up O'Malley and headed back out to the shack in the forest. They needed to look for some last clues they might have missed, then head over to Fitzgerald, Patrick, and Smith to find out the address for the Texas house.

When they finally arrived at the firm, and walked into the office, many of the staff just stared at them. At the front desk, they asked to speak to someone in charge. George Patrick came out to the front to meet them. "What can I do for you gentlemen?" He asked.

"We're Detectives Fenton and O'Malley from L.A.P.D. homicide. We need to ask you some questions about your partner, John Fitzgerald." O'Malley told the man.

"Of course, please follow me."

The men were led into Mr. Patrick's office and offered some coffee. "Thank you," Hugh told the man.

"I'll cut right to the reason we're here. I'm sure you're aware of how much trouble John Fitzgerald is in. He's our prime suspect in a murder investigation and has disappeared. We need to speak with him and clear him from this investigation. We need your help to do that."

"What can I do?" He asked.

"We've been told that Fitzgerald has a vacation home in Texas. We need you to give us the address."

"I do know that he has a residence there. But, I don't have any idea where. I can check the files to see if there is any record of it."

"Thank you, Mr. Patrick. Anything you could do would be much appreciated." Hugh responded.

While Patrick went to check the files, the men looked around. They walked into Fitzgerald's office and began to investigate. They looked at Fitzgerald's pictures, and began to open his filing cabinets. One of them was locked. "Excuse me, Miss? Do you have the key for this filing cabinet?" Hugh asked the temporary secretary.

"Yes, let me grab it for you." She responded.

The secretary brought the key in and opened the cabinet. She went back to her desk and left the detectives alone.

"Hey, look at this." O'Malley called to Hugh.

"Oh, those must be the pictures that Bobbi told us she found before." Hugh said.

"Yeah, but look at these." He opened another folder and found photos of Fitzgerald, another man, and Fitzgerald's wife. The photos seemed harmless enough, until they flipped through a few. Then they got a little strange. The photos were of Fitzgerald and his wife having sex. They were tied up, wearing bondage gear, and the other man was taking the photos. Then all three of them were in some of the photos together.

Interesting. Not only did Fitzgerald have a kinky side, but his wife was into it as well, Hugh thought. They were wondering if the other man was Sam. They would have to take the photos and pay a little visit to Mrs. Fitzgerald. It seemed that she had lied when they went to speak to her before. She had told detectives that she knew nothing of her husband's escapades and was appalled at what he was involved in. She was clearly hiding something.

Mr. Patrick came back and gave them the address. "This is the only address I have in Fitzgerald's personal file, anywhere near Texas." He said.

"Thanks so much for your help. We really appreciate it. We'll be in touch." Hugh told him, and the men left.

On the way to Fitzgerald's house to see his wife, Hugh stopped to check on Bobbi. "I'll be right back," he told O'Malley.

He knocked on the door and Bobbi opened. She smiled. "Hey baby. I'm so glad you stopped by. I was just thinking about you."

"I can't stay. We found out where Fitzgerald could possibly be staying, so I have to head out to Texas. I just wanted to come say bye and tell you I miss you."

"You're too sweet, honey. I miss you too, more than you know. Just keep in touch okay?"

"I will honey." He kissed her and was on his way.

They drove to Beverly Hills to talk to Mrs. Fitzgerald. When she opened the door, she wasn't pleased to see them. "Detectives," she said.

"Mrs. Fitzgerald. We need to ask you a few more questions." Hugh told her.

"Of course, come in."

They sat down on the sofa. "Can I offer you gentlemen some coffee or a drink?"

"No thank you. We don't have much time. We're on our way out to Texas. Just wanted to ask you about some photos we found at your husband's office."

She appeared instantly uncomfortable and knew they were moving into dangerous territory. *I was sure James put those in a safe place where no one could ever find them*, she thought.

"Ok. I'll give it a try."

Hugh showed her the photographs and the color drained from her face. She tried to remain calm. She didn't want to show them any emotion that could incriminate her or James in any way.

"What exactly would you like to know about them?" She asked calmly.

"Can you tell me who this man is?"

"I only know him as Sam."

"No last name, place of residence, anything else?" O'Malley asked her.

"No. James just used to bring him over and force me to spend time with him."

"So this wasn't your cup of tea?" Hugh asked her.

"God, no. Who do you think I am? Some kind of wild woman? I only did those things because James made me feel guilty if I didn't. He said it was my wifely duty."

"Well thanks for your time, Mrs. Fitzgerald. We have to get going. If you have any contact with James, you know what to do."

"Good day, gentlemen." She said and closed the door.

The detectives boarded a plane to Dallas for 9 p.m. from Los Angeles. It was difficult to get a flight on such short notice, but Hugh used his pull in the department to get it done. Once there, they would work with the local police department to get a vehicle and have access to the resources they needed.

They landed on time and headed for the local station. When the cab dropped them off, they went in and requested the lead homicide detective on duty.

A man came out and shook Hugh's hand. "I'm Detective Colton Sinclair. What can I do for you fella's?"

"We're Detectives Fenton and O'Malley from LAPD. We're here to look into a possible suspect we have for a series of murders in our area. You might have heard of them, they are commonly referred to as the 'Hollywood Murders.'"

"Yes, actually, I have heard of the case. Damn shame. So many beautiful girls getting rubbed out up there. What can I do to help?" He asked.

"Well, we have an address for a possible suspect, but didn't want to step on any toes or interfere in your jurisdiction. We wanted to get your support and help if possible." Hugh told him.

"Of course. I will introduce you to a few of my men and you can head out there now. Is the house in Dallas?"

"Yes. I have the address and we would like to go as soon as possible, before the suspect knows we're on to him." Hugh explained.

"Let's get going." Sinclair said.

Hugh, O'Malley, Sinclair, and a Detective Robert Smith were on the way to Fitzgerald's house about an hour later. It was dark, so the men hoped they could stake out the house a little before heading in. When they got there, however, the house was completely dark.

They sat outside for a while to see if anyone came home. There was no activity, and no one in sight. They got comfortable and knew it was going to be a long night.

Chapter 29

"Who the hell is that outside?" Fitzgerald asked.

"What are you talking about, you paranoid freak?"

"I just went upstairs and there are two cars parked across the street from the house, and no one is getting out of them."

"Maybe they got out before you knew the cars were there?"

"No. I've been sitting outside and no one was there an hour ago." Fitz said.

The men were in the basement of the house. They had decided to leave the lights off in the main house so in case they were discovered, no one would know they were there.

"Oh, don't be afraid honey. We're here to have some fun." Sam told the redhead looking at him. She had duck tape over her mouth, was dressed only in her panties and bra and had been crying. She had burn marks from a cigarette on her arms and legs. She had been down in the basement for at least two days and was exhausted.

"I'm telling you man. It doesn't look right. You need to come check it out." Fitz was beginning to get agitated.

"Fine, Fitz. Of course, you can't do anything yourself. You're coming with me. You can't have her to yourself." Sam told him angrily.

They walked upstairs and left the girl lying on the table in the basement. They peeked outside through the window and saw the two cars. "Damn, looks like cop cars." Sam said.

"I told you! What should we do?" Fitz began to panic.

"Well they have no idea we're here or they would have already come in. We need to get out of here, though. They've found out about the house and we need to move.

We'll stay in the basement until tomorrow morning, dispose of the girl, then head out after they leave."

Hugh and the men stayed out there all night and found nothing. Maybe Hugh had been wrong to think Fitzgerald had come all the way out here. It was, after all just a hunch. Maybe Gambini was trying to throw them off? Maybe he was more involved than he let on. Was Hugh being naïve to think that a man like Gambini would try to help them solve this case?

He had to check while he was here just to rule it out. They went up to the door while the other two men searched the back of the house. Hugh rang the doorbell but there was no answer. They looked around the side of the house, but still saw nothing out of the ordinary. Detective Sinclair yelled for Hugh.

The men went running around the back of the house. "What is it?" Hugh asked.

"I think we might have found something here." Sinclair responded.

There was a door down to a basement at the back of the house. There was a harsh smell coming from the door and there were footprints all around the entrance. "Damn! If they were in this house the entire time and we sat out there like idiots…"

Hugh was interrupted, "What is that?" Sinclair asked.

"Oh shit. That looks like blood spots," O'Malley investigated.

The men raised their guns and headed into the basement. "Police! Come out with your hands up." Sinclair yelled.

No one made a sound. It looked like the basement was empty. The men walked down the steps carefully using their flashlights. "No one down here, boss." Sinclair's other detective, Smith confirmed.

As the men walked down into the basement, they were knocked over by the strong smell of death. It was clear there were bodies here. Hugh saw the same setup he had seen at the shack in Los Angeles: a surgical table with large lights and many tools around it. There was also a television, a refrigerator, couch, and torture devices. The blood spots were on the stairs and throughout the room. There were cigarette butts everywhere and empty beer bottles. Some of the surgical tools left behind still had remains of skin on them.

"Smitty, go call for backup so we can process this scene before we touch anything." Sinclair said.

It was only a matter of time before backup arrived, so Hugh wanted to have a look around for any clues right away. He picked up a photo on the floor. He held it between his two fingers careful not to touch it or remove prints and saw a beautiful, young redhead. "You might want to check this out and run it through your database of missing girls, Detective Sinclair."

"I don't have to. That's Vivien Claussen. She's been missing for a couple days. She was believed to be kidnapped from the local coffee shop. Her parents have been worried sick about her and even offered a reward." He responded.

"Damn. I hate this part," He said. It just breaks my heart to have to tell the parents that their baby has been found dead. And, not just dead, but tortured."

"Well, technically, we haven't found her yet, just her picture." Hugh told him.

"True, but I don't put much faith into her being found alive."

Backup arrived and the men began to search the scene. They looked throughout the yard, trying to discover the body. They had no idea what they would find, they continued to dig in several places, but luckily no bodies were unearthed.

"At the last scene, he buried the victims. Where could she be?" Hugh asked.

"We found something here!" One of the officers called out.

The men ran over to the back area by the basement. There was an old freezer there that had been rusted so badly, no one had paid much attention to it. The officer opened the freezer and there was Vivien Claussen. She had only been dead a few hours and was shoved into the freezer so sloppily, it was clear the men had been in a hurry to flee the scene.

"Once again, we have a victim with the name of an actress. It has to be the same guy." Hugh said. "I just don't understand how he got away without us seeing him last night."

"It looks like there are two sets of footprints here." One of the officers commented.

"I knew he was here with Sam," Hugh responded.

"Who's Sam?" Detective Sinclair asked. "I thought you only had one suspect."

"We do that we are very sure of, but there has been a man who we can't seem to locate or even name throughout the investigation. He had to have been the one here with Fitzgerald."

The men continued to process the scene while Hugh formulated a plan for his next move.

Bobbi was so worried about Hugh. He hadn't called her since he left for Dallas. She was trying to keep herself busy, but since she wasn't working, she was going a little stir crazy. She had been visiting Charlie every day, and trying to help him with the kids. His kids were great. They loved their daddy more than anything and were actually adapting to their mother's death quite well.

Bobbi hadn't been feeling well since she got out of the hospital. It had been a really tough month. The only good thing to come out of it all was her relationship with Hugh. She knew he was her soul mate. She ached for him when he wasn't around. She needed to do some laundry and other chores, but felt really nauseous. Just then the phone rang.

"Hello?" She answered.

"Hey baby." It was Hugh.

"I'm so glad you called," she said. "I've been so worried about you."

"I'm fine. We've just been really busy since we got into town. Things are not looking good over here. Fitzgerald is at it again and he took off. I might have to stay here a few more days until we get it all sorted out."

"I miss you so much, honey, but take your time. I know this case is extremely important."

"I miss you too baby. I better go. The guys are calling me. I will give you a call tomorrow ok?"

They hung up. Bobbi had to run to the bathroom. She didn't feel good and began to panic a little. She had been in the hospital a few times with head injuries and she hoped she wasn't sick or something. She went to lie down for a while.

Chapter 30

Charlie woke up from a nap and felt unbelievable sadness. It had been two weeks since Shirley was found, and he still couldn't get out of bed. He tried so hard for the kids, but felt he had nothing to live for without her. His parents, Hugh, and even Bobbi tried every day to encourage him, but nothing worked.

He was on some medication to get him through the day, but he no longer needed it since he had been drinking. Gin was getting him through his days, and quite well actually. He felt like such a failure. Not only had he lost his wife, but he couldn't get out of bed, and now he was drinking himself to death.

It didn't matter if he was feeling sorry for himself. He was allowed. His wife had just died for Christ's sake! No one was going to tell him when he should move on. He wanted to give the department a big "fuck you." They told him he had one more week to get back to work, or they were going to have to let him go. What kind of support was that? What a crock of shit! He had been there for years and that was how they were going to treat him?

He was so angry that most people didn't even recognize him anymore. His parents were constantly telling him he needed to get back to church and spend more time with the family. Why should I go to church? He wondered. God took his wife from him. He no longer wanted anything to do with God. Why should he go listen to the pastor speak when he didn't believe anything he said? God answers prayers. Yeah, right.

The phone rang and it was Hugh. "Hey buddy. How are you feeling?"

"I'm fine Hugh. I told you to stop checking up on me."

"I'm not. I just wanted to update you on the case." Hugh told him.

"We found another body. The house in Texas has been abandoned and the men are on the move again. We now know that Fitzgerald and Sam are working together. We're close, but in the meantime, you have to get yourself together so you can go back to work."

"You know what Hugh? I'll go back to work when I'm damned good and ready. No one is going to tell me how long I should mourn my wife, especially not you."

"What's that supposed to mean?" Hugh asked.

"Nothing, it's just that you have Bobbi and I have no one. I'm sorry. I didn't mean to take my frustrations out on you, I'm just tired."

"Alright buddy, take it easy. I'll call you tomorrow."

They hung up and Charlie almost kicked himself for what he was about to say to his friend. He had promised himself that he would never tell Hugh about the brief affair with Bobbi, and in the middle of his own misery, he almost did.

Charlie climbed out of bed, threw away the bottle of gin, and went to take a shower. It was time to get back to his life.

Bobbi hadn't felt right for the entire week. She decided to go to the doctor to have her head checked. She thought she might have a concussion. The doctor came back into the room after examining her, and said, "Bobbi, when was the last time you had your period?"

Bobbi just looked at him. "I'm sorry, what?"

"Your monthly cycle, honey. Have you been late?"

Bobbi couldn't remember the last time she had had one. With everything going on, it had been the last thing on her mind. "I guess it's been a couple of months. I hadn't noticed with being in the hospital and everything going on. Why?"

"Well because you're pregnant." The doctor told her.

Bobbi just stared at him in shock. Tears began to well up in her eyes and she couldn't wait to tell Hugh. A baby wasn't something they planned, but she knew he would be so excited. *Oh my God,* She thought.

"How far along am I?" She asked the doctor.

"Could be anywhere from one to two months. We don't know the exact time yet."

The doctor looked back over his shoulder just as Bobbi was falling to the floor.

Sam had stolen a new car from the grocery store parking lot. "Let's go!" He yelled at Fitzgerald. "We need to get moving."

They were on their way back to Arizona. There had been some beautiful women there, and no one seemed to notice when they were new in town. They planned to stay in a hotel until they could find a place to rent.

They pulled into the gas station and picked up some cigarettes. Sam went to use the payphone and asked the operator to connect him to the LAPD. When the connection came through, he asked for Detective Brower. "I'm sorry, sir. Detective Brower is out on leave this week. Is there anything I can do for you?" The desk sergeant asked.

"No, can you just leave him a message? Let him know Sam called to say hi and see how he's doing."

"Ok, will do, sir. Any phone number to return the call?"

"No, not right now. He'll know what to do." The line went dead.

Charlie decided to go into the station for a bit. When he walked in, the desk sergeant handed him his messages and said, "It's good to see you back, man."

Charlie had felt that it was time. He needed to get his mind back on the case so he could help solve these murders. He had to help make the streets safe again for others, so nothing like what happened to Shirley could happen to another family.

He headed toward his desk. It was nice to be back, actually. "Hey Charlie. Good to see you, Pal. Do you need anything?" One of the detectives called out.

"No, I'm good Paul. Just glad to be back."

He sat down at his desk and read his messages. Mostly updates from Hugh. Some messages from Bobbi checking in. Others from the coroner updating him on the bodies of the eighteen girls. He froze when he came to the next message. "I'll be damned," he said. *That son of a bitch has got some balls*, he thought. He had actually called the station looking for Charlie. He hadn't left a number but said he would call back. Charlie swore he would sit at his desk all night if that's what it took to speak to this scumbag.

He asked dispatch to connect him to Hugh so he could tell him about it.

"Fenton here."

"Hugh, it's Charlie. I just got to the office and there's a message from Sam here."

"What?"

"Yeah, he just said to tell me he called, and would call back. I'm going to sit here all night if I have to. I will get back to you as soon as I know something."

"Sounds good, buddy. Oh, by the way, Charlie. Good to have you back."

Sam and Fitz decided to head out for a drink. They needed to blow off some steam. They went into a dive bar called *The Watering Hole*. The place was a dump. There were no attractive women anywhere and it was very dark. It had to do. It was the only place they could walk to.

"What'll it be?" The bartender asked.

"Two beers." Sam answered.

People were staring at them. Maybe it wasn't such a good idea to go to a local's only place. They might be remembered later. Oh well. It was time to loosen up, and have some fun.

The hours passed by and the men became more drunk. They were starting to want some female attention, so when one of the women approached them at the bar, they started flirting with her.

"Hey boys." She was slurring a little, and her dress kept falling open in the front. "You want to spend some time with me?"

"Depends on what you mean by spend some time," Sam answered.

"I think you know what I mean. I have a girlfriend over there too if you all want to come over to our table."

The three of them went over to the table and sat down. "Ruth, this here's—wait what did you say your names were?"

"I'm James and this is Sam. And you ladies are?"

"I'm Anne and this here is Ruth."

"Pleasure to meet you ladies. Can we order you another drink?" Fitz asked them.

They nodded. "Bartender, another round over here." Fitz told the man.

The four of them started cutting up and really enjoying themselves. Fitz kept giving Sam the "let's go" look, but Sam had other plans.

Sam excused himself and went to the payphone outside.

When the woman answered, Sam said, "Detective Brower, please."

The phone rang and Charlie practically jumped up the minute it did. "Detective Brower." He answered.

"Oh goodie, Detective Brower, so nice to finally hear your voice, friend."

"Who is this?"

"This is Sam."

"First of all, you piece of shit, I'm not your friend."

"Awe come on Detective. Don't be so short. You might want to be nice to me."

"Why on earth would I want to do that? I want to rip your heart out and feed it to you before I run you over with my car."

"Ouch. Harsh. Is this about Shirley?"

Charlie could feel himself losing control. He would not let this low life get to him. "What do you want Sam?"

"Just wanted to tell you that we're not through yet. We have a few more girls to spend time with. We've left Texas and are on our way back. I really don't think you and your team are smart enough to catch us. But, I just wanted to let you know."

"You are some piece of work. Don't worry, we will catch you, you can bet on it. I won't rest until I do."

The line went dead.

Chapter 31

Hugh was on his way back to Los Angeles. He had thanked Detective Sinclair and his men for all their help and was on his way. The trip to Texas hadn't been overly successful and it was time to get back on track. Charlie was back so they would have an extra pair of hands on the case. He missed Bobbi so much. He couldn't wait to hold her, touch her, and kiss her. He was shocked at himself that he cared about her this much already. He actually believed he loved her. He nodded off and slept until they landed.

Charlie picked them up at the airport and the three started debriefing each other right away. Hugh could not believe that Sam had called Charlie to tell him they were on their way back to Los Angeles. "What a sick son of a bitch. It's like he's just taunting us." Hugh said.

"Yeah, but at the same time, it's like he wants us to find them." Charlie responded.

"I don't know about that, but we'll take whatever help we can right now. This case needs to be closed before any more girls die." Hugh said.

Bobbi sat in the apartment a nervous wreck. She was waiting for Hugh to come over. She hadn't seen him since last week and missed him terribly. *What will he say about the pregnancy? Will he be happy? Will he be angry about her and Charlie?* She wondered. She had to tell him the truth about everything. It was the only chance she had to save her relationship. She had to be honest or it would never work.

Hugh arrived and Bobbi let him in. He kissed her and told her how glad he was to see her. "I've missed you so much babe."

"I've missed you too. More than you know."

Bobbi looked tired. She had a lot on her mind. "Are you ok, honey?" Hugh asked her.

"I need to talk to you about something, Hugh. Can you sit down with me?"

"Of course. What is it, darling? You know you can tell me anything."

"I'm pregnant." She just blurted it out before she even knew what she was saying.

Hugh jumped up and hugged her. "Are you sure?" He asked her.

"Yes, I'm sure. I went to the doctor yesterday and they told me."

"Oh, honey, I'm thrilled."

Bobbi didn't want to tell him the rest. But, she had to. It was the only thing to do.

"Hugh, I don't want to hurt you. I hope you will hear me out before you jump to conclusions. Before you and I met, I had a brief affair with someone. By brief, I mean one time. It meant nothing. It was something that happened because I was confused about what I was involved in with Howard. I made a terrible judgment call, but I fixed it and was never with this man again."

"Ok. Why are you telling me this Bobbi?"

"There is a slight chance the baby could be his."

Hugh just stared at her. He was clearly hurt and didn't know how to respond. He got up and walked into the kitchen.

"Hugh, please come sit back down." She continued. "I love you. You have to know that. I've never felt this way about any man before. I want a future with you. I don't want anything that happened in the past to jeopardize that. You have to remember that this all happened before I even knew you."

"Who is this man, Bobbi? Do you still have contact with him?" He was getting angrier by the minute.

Bobbi didn't know how to say it, so she just did. "It's Charlie, Hugh."

Hugh thought he heard her incorrectly. "I'm sorry, I thought you said it was Charlie."

"I did." She began to cry when she saw how hurt he was.

He looked like someone had punched him in the stomach. "Wow, Bobbi. You get around huh?" He started walking toward the door.

"Hugh, wait. That's not fair. I told you the truth. Do you know how difficult this is for me? I'm taking a huge chance of losing the only man I've ever loved. Doesn't that mean anything to you?"

"Right now, no." He turned and walked out of the apartment.

Bobbi sat down on the sofa and cried while she tried to figure out what to do.

Hugh drove as fast as he could back to the station. *How could they do this to him? He trusted both of them. The entire time they had all three been together, had they had feelings for one another?* All these thoughts were racing through Hugh's mind. He felt so stupid that he had loved a woman who clearly didn't love him. *How could she love him if she had been with his best friend only weeks before they met?*

He couldn't wait to confront Charlie. After all he did for him, he couldn't believe Charlie had withheld this from him. They were partners. He should have told him from the beginning and Hugh could have decided if he wanted to get involved with Bobbi or not.

He practically ran into the station and asked one of the detectives where Charlie was. The man pointed toward the restroom. Hugh walked over there and saw Charlie. "Hey, Hugh, I was just about to call you…" was all he got out before Hugh punched him right in the face. Charlie went down to the floor and looked shocked.

"What the hell is going on Hugh? What was that for?"

"You know damn well what that's for. You slept with Bobbi and didn't even tell me? I thought we were closer than that, Charlie. You both deserve each other."

Everyone in the station was watching the scene take place. They were all in awe. They had never even seen the two men argue, let alone have a physical altercation. Hugh walked out of the station and Charlie got up off the floor. Everyone went back to work and didn't ask any questions. Charlie went to the bathroom to wipe off his face.

Bobbi must have told him. But why? Charlie wondered. They had agreed to keep the hurtful information from Hugh because they felt it was best for all involved. Charlie wondered if they had made a mistake. He had to talk to Bobbi to find out what had happened.

Charlie went back to his desk and called Bobbi. She had been crying when she answered the phone. She sounded hopeful. "Hugh?"

"No, Bobbi. It's Charlie. I'm sorry. What happened Bobbi? I thought we agreed not to tell him."

"I wasn't going to Charlie, but I'm pregnant and there is a chance it could be your baby. I thought he had a right to know. I love him too much for him to not know the truth."

Charlie tried to process what she just said. "Bobbi, did you say that the baby might be mine?"

"Yes, Charlie. I'm sorry. I know we were only together once and the chances are slim, but there is still a chance."

"Well, you did the right thing by telling him. He needs to know the truth. I know it's not mine, but I appreciate you being honest about everything. In the meantime, we have to fix this. Your boyfriend and my best friend is out there upset and might do something stupid. I think I know where he might be. I will go try to find him and call you when I do ok?"

"Thanks so much Charlie. I truly love him and can't lose him over this. Please let me know when you find him."

Chapter 32

Charlie left the station in a hurry. He wanted to find Hugh to explain before he got crazy ideas in his head. They were like brothers. Hugh had been there for him more than anyone else when Shirley died and he couldn't have him feeling like Charlie had betrayed his trust.

Charlie pulled into the parking lot of *The Hideaway*, a local dive bar that they very rarely visited. It was the place they went when they didn't feel like talking. He saw Hugh's car when he pulled in and got out. When Charlie peeked in the front door, Hugh was sitting alone on the barstool. He didn't look good. He actually looked really angry, and Charlie wondered if he should even approach him.

He walked over to the bar and told the bartender, "I'll have what he's having and give him another."

"How'd you find me?" Hugh asked.

"It wasn't hard, Hugh. You don't drink often and I know you pretty well."

"Obviously not well enough to tell me you slept with my girlfriend."

Charlie let the comment die. He sat down and took a few sips of his drink. The silence between them was good for now. The two looked up at the game on television and just sat. After a good 30 minutes, Hugh looked at him and asked, "Why didn't you tell me?"

"Hugh, neither one of us wanted to tell you because we knew how happy you were and we didn't think our one night stand should matter. It didn't mean anything for either of us. I told you all about it before. I was upset with Shirley and needed someone to talk to. She was distraught over what she was going through with Howard. We met and that's it. We never met up again, and we both knew it was a huge mistake."

"I just don't think I can sleep with someone my best friend has been with."

"Look, Hugh. I understand and you have to do what you think is right, but I can guarantee you that neither of us has feelings for the other. It would be a shame to let someone so perfect for you go because of pride."

"Well, what if the baby is yours?"

"Hugh, we both know that's not possible. Or maybe you don't, but I can't have any more children."

Hugh just stared at him. "Really? I didn't know that."

"I talked to Bobbi a bit ago and didn't tell her either. I thought you should be the one to discuss it with her. It's none of my business. You two are perfect for each other and shouldn't let this stop your happiness. You're going to have a baby, Hugh."

Hugh was so mad about the whole situation that he completely forgot about the baby. "I'm going to have a baby, Charlie!"

"I know, buddy. I'm so happy for you. Let's have a drink to celebrate!"

The two men had one more drink, then Charlie told Hugh he would call Bobbi to let her know he found him.

"Bobbi? I found him at a local bar and we're ok. I'm having a drink with him, and he says he will call you when he's done."

Bobbi was grateful and felt better after she hung up.

The two men left the bar after a few cups of coffee and Hugh headed over to Bobbi's apartment. He knew what he had to do.

He rang the doorbell and she came to the door. "Who is it?" She asked.

"It's Hugh baby. Can I come in?"

She opened the door and let him in. As soon as she did, he grabbed her and kissed her so passionately her knees went weak.

When he let her go, she was crying. "Does this mean we're ok, baby?" She asked him.

"We're better than ok." He got down on his knee. "Bobbi Brooks, will you marry me?"

She started crying again, looked at him and simply said, "yes."

They spent the night together talking about the baby, their marriage, and the future.

Charlie felt so much better after he got home. He went in to check on the kids, kissed them, tucked them in, and finally headed to bed. He lie awake for a while thinking about how funny life was. He missed Shirley terribly, but for the first time since she died, he felt optimistic about the future. *Things are going to be okay*, he thought. He prayed that night for the first time since she died. He thanked God for all the blessings he was given and asked Him to help Charlie be a better man.

Chapter 33

The men were on their way back to the hotel with the two women when one of them passed out. "Oh Jesus. What the hell do we do with her, now?" Fitzgerald asked. "She can't even walk. What good is she going to be to us?" The other woman was barely walking herself and kept stumbling while trying to smoke her cigarette.

"Come on sweetheart. Let's go up the stairs." Sam guided her as Fitz carried the other woman over his shoulder. Once they got into the room, they put both women on the beds while they came up with a plan of action. Both women were passed out and easy targets.

"This isn't even fun anymore." Sam said. "They aren't terrified, they aren't challenging, and they sure as hell ain't attractive."

"What are you saying, Sam?"

"I'm saying get them the hell out of here and tomorrow we'll go back to L.A. where we can find some real nice pieces of ass."

"You're serious?"

"As a heart attack. Now get them out of here. They make me sick."

Fitz woke the girls up, took them downstairs and left them on the curb outside the hotel. They could find their own way home. They were spared their lives tonight. They didn't deserve anything else. He sure as hell wasn't going to make sure they got home safely, that's for damn sure.

When Fitz came back to the hotel room, he wanted to find out what was wrong with Sam. He had been acting strange since they got to Texas.

"What's wrong with you lately?"

"Just because I didn't want to screw around with some hideous broad, there's something wrong with me?" He responded.

"No, it's not just that. You seem a little preoccupied lately and it's starting to make me nervous. You don't have any ideas of trying to sell me out to save yourself now do ya Sam?"

"Yeah that's it. Come on Fitz, drop it. I just want to get back to L.A. as quickly as possible."

The two men went to bed and couldn't wait to get up and head back to sunny California in the morning.

Charlie and Hugh had been trying feverishly to find out about this Sam guy. No one knew anything about him. Or maybe no one wanted to tell them anything about him. They paid a visit to Carlton again to see if he had any new information.

"None guys. I'm sorry. I wish I could help you. The only thing I can think of is you might want to ask around Chinatown. Those guys had a lot of drug deals down there. Someone might want to sell him out for a good price."

"Thanks Carlton. We'll be in touch," Charlie told him.

They drove out to Chinatown and began showing the photos around to as many people as they could. They told the kids in the neighborhood that if they could give them any information about the man in the photo, they would pay them well for it. So far, they weren't having much luck. Everyone wanted to help, but it was like Sam was a ghost. No one knew anything about him.

They were so frustrated. They had been at it all day. "Time for lunch," Hugh suggested. "Yeah, let's get something to restart us."

They stopped into Mr. Chang's for some of the best Chow Mein this side of China. As they ate, they discussed the case. The clues were right in front of them, but they just couldn't see them.

"Someone around here knows him. Maybe they're afraid of him." Charlie suggested.

The waiter came over to check on them and seemed agitated and quickly walked away. "What's his problem?" Hugh asked.

"No idea. That was weird." Charlie looked down and realized the photos of Sam were sitting on the table. "I think he knows Sam." Charlie told Hugh.

The two men got up and walked toward the kitchen were the man was hiding.

"We need to talk to you." Charlie told him.

"I know nothing." The man said.

"Can we go somewhere you feel safe to talk?" Hugh asked him.

"Ok, we go upstairs."

They headed upstairs to a small apartment above the restaurant. The man was shaking and was very reluctant to talk to Charlie and Hugh.

"You know this man?" Charlie asked him.

He nodded. He didn't want to say anything else.

"How do you know him?"

"He is bad man." The waiter said.

"We know that. Can you tell me about him?"

"Please, we need to find him. Girls are dying and we believe he's the reason." Hugh added.

The waiter motioned for the men to sit down and he began to tell the story.

Sam was Samuel Hanson. He came here from San Francisco about a year ago and began running with some bad people. He had been into petty crime in San Francisco, but nothing like what he was into down here.

In San Francisco, Samuel grew up in a wealthy suburb where he wanted for nothing. His parents spoiled him, educating him at the best schools, providing music lessons by the best teachers, and allowing him to get away with pretty much anything he wanted.

Sam was bored. He began to resent the hoity toity life he had to be a part of. He wanted to experience things. He was looking for a little excitement in his life. So, he dropped out of school, started hanging out with the wrong crowd, became a greaser, and headed down to L.A.

Los Angeles was like a dream. When Sam got here, he didn't know where to begin. The possibilities were endless. Anyone could make money or be famous here. Hollywood was like paradise. Gorgeous girls, plenty of money, and people into some kinky shit, and he was only too happy to provide it for them.

Since he didn't have much money to start with, he moved into a small apartment in Chinatown. He was well liked at first by the people of the town. He seemed friendly, polite, and was a good tipper. But this was all an act just to gain the trust of the people.

Girls in the area were getting attacked and even raped. The people began to blame the new outsider. Sam had some small drug dealings with the boys in the town, so he used that as leverage to avoid people going to the police.

Eventually, he began a relationship with one of the daughters in the town. Her name was Lindy. She was beautiful. Long, straight hair and gorgeous brown eyes. Every boy in the area wanted to marry her. She was sweet, fun, and had the reputation for being good in bed.

Sam had to have her. He began to give her pills when they were making love to "enhance" the experience. Before long, she was hooked on them. She couldn't function without them. She was completely dependent upon Sam. The men in the town hated him for it.

Before long, he talked Lindy into letting another man have his way with her while he watched. She didn't want to at first, but after giving her the pills, she would do anything Sam wanted.

That led to Sam suggesting they get paid for her to be with other men. Sam was pimping her out. Everyone in the town knew it, but Lindy was so in love with Sam and his drugs that she did whatever he asked of her.

Lindy had a lot of beautiful friends who were also in need of money. They saw the clothes Lindy wore, the smile on her face, and the attractive boyfriend she had. She seemed to have it all. Lindy had no problem convincing them to prostitute themselves. They came to her.

Sam and Lindy were getting rich and business kept getting better and better. It was time to go more call girl service, rather than cheap whore on a street corner.

One night, Sam and Lindy were having sex, when he decided to try to choke her. She was into it. She loved to try new things. She started to kick and scream. She couldn't breathe, but Sam didn't stop. He was getting turned on watching her struggle. He finally stopped, just short of killing her. Lindy was afraid of him from that moment on.

Each time they were making love, Lindy wondered if he would go too far. She didn't want to be alone with him. He was becoming more and more controlling and even began hitting her. Once when they were making love, he took his cigarette and burned her on the stomach.

He also started having sex with the other girls at this point. Lindy didn't say anything because she was afraid. She was also hoping he would find one of the other women to be with so he would grow tired of her. He never did though. His connection to Lindy was deep, or so he said.

One night as they were making love, he tried to choke her again. She began to panic, writhing around in pain. He began laughing at this and continued to choke her. He wouldn't stop this time and ended up killing the poor girl.

He had to hide the body. He was surprised at himself that he wasn't ashamed of what he did. He had no remorse. He was sad he couldn't be with her anymore, but not sad she was dead. He rolled her body up into the floor rug and carried her out to his car the next morning. He drove her body out to the Angeles National Forest and buried her there. No one would ever find her, he thought.

He returned to town and no one noticed she was gone for a few days. After that, people began to get suspicious. Everyone was so fearful of him, though, that no one dare to ask Sam where she was. Her parents put a reward out for her, but never contacted the police. She was never seen or heard from again.

The townspeople knew Sam was responsible for her death but couldn't prove anything. He controlled so much of the town now with his drugs, gambling, and prostitution that the people needed his connections.

His call girl business was doing well. He had men calling him willing to pay big bucks for an Asian girl. They had fantasies that their wives were not willing to act out. They called Sam, Sam met them at a local hotel, the girls did their thing, and that was it. It was an easy way to make a living.

Sam started encountering problems when he had to involve some of the local crime bosses of the area. He didn't really know the men, but saw Sam was making good money and wanted a piece of the action. That's when he decided it was time to get out of it. He pretty much handed over the business to the girls. He left Chinatown and began living in Hollywood. He still had a craving for rough sex, so he started calling his old contacts for girls. But, this way, he could have them, rough them up a little, and be done with it.

After a while, it wasn't enough to just rough them up. He wanted to watch them suffer like Lindy had. Just thinking about what he had done to her turned him on. He called up Howard Starks one night and asked him for a beautiful girl who had an actresses' first name. Howard set it up and they met at the Roosevelt. When he got there,

there were three girls for him to choose from. It worked out well.

The next time, they met at the Knickerbocker. Things got a little out of hand and he ended up killing the girl. He had Howard's guys help him dispose of the body for five hundred dollars each. No questions asked. Howard didn't like that his guys were involved in it and told Sam he wouldn't clean up his messes again. That's when he had to find someone else to do the dirty work.

James Fitzgerald used to come to Sam in Chinatown for girls. His wife wasn't into anything unusual, so he wanted a woman to act out his fantasies with. He found Sam. Throughout the months, Sam began to get a lot of dirt on Fitzgerald, or Fitz as he called him. The man was into some sick shit. He was partner in a local law firm and would be ruined if anyone found out about his fetishes. He trusted Sam to be discreet. Sam used this to blackmail him.

At first, Sam told Fitz he wanted him to help dispose of some trash he couldn't unload himself. Fitz agreed. What choice did he have? When he showed up that night and Sam showed him the dead body, Fitz freaked out and told him he wanted no part of it. "That's fine," Sam said. "I guess your firm will know what you do on the weekends." That's all Sam had to say and Fitz was in.

They took the bodies up to the Angeles National Forest that night. Sam had started creating a hideaway for his torture victims in a shack up there. Fitz was interested and turned on by the process of killing a woman in the heat of passion.

Sam told Fitz all about it and convinced him to take part in one of the murders. Fitz tried it and loved it. He had no remorse. He was so excited to do it again, that he was constantly bothering Sam about the next time.

Sam was bored with it and needed the next high, so that's when he began leaving the bodies in local parts of Hollywood. He needed someone to know what he was doing, even if they didn't know it was him. He wanted to have the police after him, to prove he was just that much smarter than they were. Once he found out the main detective on the case had a hard on for him, he was thrilled. It became a game.

Each day, Fitz and Sam came up with new ways to torture their victims. They burned them with cigarettes, raped them with objects, made them touch each other, cut them with surgical instruments, and other horrible things. The only thing that made each one worth it, though was hearing them beg for their lives.

Charlie and Hugh left in a hurry after getting as much information as they could on Sam. They began searching the database for a last known address. They drove out to an apartment building on Hollywood and Vine. The landlord said he hadn't seen Sam in a few days. They got the man to open the apartment up and right away they recognized the familiar stench. "Oh Jesus!" Hugh shouted. "Go call for an ambulance and tell them to bring the coroner," he instructed the landlord.

Hugh and Charlie walked into the apartment while covering their faces. "Where is it?" Hugh asked.

Charlie shrugged. "Let's check out the bedroom." He suggested.

There was nothing there. The men began to look around the apartment for anything that could be of use to them. They found an address book, some family photos, and various sex/torture toys. They spotted a small pool of blood on the floor by the bathroom. "What the hell?" Charlie said.

They both looked up and realized it was dripping from the vent. The body had to be up there. Once again, this piece of shit has left a poor girl dead like this. They didn't want to climb up into the crawl space, so they waited for the coroner.

Once the coroner got there, the men got a stepladder and removed the woman. She was Latina, gorgeous, and had no clothes on. She had been dead approximately 2 weeks. She had no marks that could identify her and she was bloated from being stuck up in the vent. Her poor parents or family members would have to identify her like this.

It was time for Charlie and Hugh to get going. They needed to find out where these monsters were heading.

Chapter 34

They pulled into a local motel just outside of Hollywood after the long drive. "Finally, we're here." Sam said.

"Home, sweet home." Added Fitz.

They were exhausted from the long drive and decided to call it a night. They made sure to give false information to the desk clerk of the motel, telling him they were traveling salesmen. They just wanted sleep tonight and tomorrow would be so much fun.

Charlie drove home after a very long day. He felt like they accomplished a lot and Shirley would be proud of him. He said a silent prayer of thanks for the clues they were given today. Tomorrow would be better. They were getting close to solving this case, he could just feel it. Once that happened, his wife could truly be at peace.

Hugh drove home to Bobbi. They were getting married next weekend and there was a lot to do. She was so excited every time she saw him come through the door, that she just lit up. It made him feel so lucky to have her to come home to every day. Things were going well for all of them. Now if they could just solve this case.

The papers announced the headline, "Hollywood Murderer back in Hollywood!" Charlie thought he was seeing things. He stopped to look at the paper on his way into the coffee shop. He put the coin in and pulled the paper out. "Oh Jesus," he said.

He ran to the payphone and called Hugh at Bobbi's house. "Hugh, have you seen this morning's paper? Hugh said no. Well you better take a look and meet me at the coffee shop right away."

When Hugh showed up, he was completely out of breath. "How did this happen? Hugh asked Charlie.

"How did the press find out about the body before we did?" Did you call the station to find out who the hell is processing this? Hugh asked.

"No, but the paper says O'Malley was in charge. Why weren't we called last night?"

"No idea, but it sounds like we need to go talk to the Captain."

When Charlie and Hugh walked into the station, there was a quick hush. It seemed that everyone stopped what they were doing to watch them enter. They walked straight toward the Captain's office. He saw them and motioned for them to come in and close the door.

"What's going on here Cap?" Charlie asked.

"You've both been removed from the case." He responded.

"What?" Both men said in unison.

"I'm sorry guys but there is no movement in this case, bodies are appearing everywhere, and Charlie, we both know that you are too close to this. I should have taken you off this case a long time ago."

"That's bullshit and you know it Captain. Hugh and I are doing everything we can for this case. We've been working around the clock, and now you just take it and give it to O'Malley?"

"Sorry, guys. The big boys expect me to wrap this up. You've had enough time to do it and still nothing. I need more progress."

"Look, Cap, just give Charlie and I a week. We are onto some really good leads right now and are making tons of progress. If you just give us some time, we won't let you down."

He thought about it. "My ass is on the line here boys. You have to get this wrapped up by next week or you're off. Is that clear?"

"Yes, thanks Cap. We won't let you down," Charlie said.

They left the office and headed down to the coroner's office to see the body. They weren't able to process the scene so they needed to talk to O'Malley to see what he found as well.

"Nothing new guys. Same MO. Just noticing that the bodies are getting a little more beaten up. Poor girl. Cigarette burns all over her body. This one was olive skinned with darker hair. Seems like there is really no rhyme or reason for which girls he picks." O'Malley told the men.

"Great. He's not partial to any type. That makes it a lot more difficult to typecast his victims and prepare them. Anyone is a target. We do know now that Fitzgerald and Sam are working together, so keep your eye out for two men, not one." Hugh said.

"We have to get this wrapped up and catch this bastard. Too many girls are dying." O'Malley responded.

Sam was tired of Fitz. He was slowing him down. He wanted to work alone. He began thinking of a plan to get rid of him.

"What do you think, Sam? Should we go out tonight?" Fitz asked him.

Sam was glad the press was covering the murder and announcing to the city that he was back. You would think that women would be much more careful with the headlines out there, but they weren't. Women were very naïve. They trusted men too much.

"Yeah, we're going out tonight, but I'm not sure when or where. Sit tight and relax. You're driving me crazy." Sam responded.

Charlie, Hugh, and O'Malley turned the corner and saw the two men dropping the body. "Are you kidding me?" O'Malley yelled. "They're right there!"

Charlie sped up and the men got into their car and took off. Leaving a body on the streets wasn't going to work, so they called for backup to go process the body right away. They took off on a high-speed chase through Hollywood trying to catch the two men.

They rounded the corner of Hollywood and Vine about 60 mph and went up on two wheels. Charlie knew this was their only chance to stop these mad men. He had to stay with them.

In the other car, Sam was laughing. He enjoyed the chase. It was exciting. He knew that the Detectives wouldn't catch them. They were too smart for some dumb cops. Fitz was screaming in his ear. "Oh, Jesus, Sam. They're going to catch us and give us the gas chamber!"

"If you don't shut the hell up, you won't have to worry about that." Sam responded.

Sam knew that if they were caught, Fitz would tell the cops anything they wanted to know to save himself. He was a coward. He made Sam sick.

The men continued on narrowly avoiding pedestrians crossing the street. Many people ran in terror. They were shocked at what they were seeing.

"Charlie don't lose them!" Hugh yelled.

"I won't. This is for Shirley. They are getting the gas!" He responded.

They turned the corner and found the car stopped in the middle of the street. "What the hell?" Charlie asked.

Sam was outside the car with a gun pointed at Fitz. They had crashed into the wall and had a flat tire. Fitz was crying like a big baby.

Charlie, Hugh, and O'Malley got out. All three men had their guns drawn, ready to shoot these two sick bastards. It took everything Charlie had in him not to shoot them both right then and there to end it all.

"Put your gun down, Sam. We know all about everything and you have no way out." Hugh yelled.

"Hell no, this is too much fun. I love seeing you gentlemen chase your tails around this city." Sam responded.

Fitz was still crying hysterically, begging Sam to take the gun off him.

"Shut up you damn coward," Sam told him.

This didn't look good for Fitz. They had to do everything they could to save him so he could pay for his crimes later.

Right then, Sam looked at the men, smiled an evil smile, put the gun to Fitz' head, and pulled the trigger. He dropped like a sack of potatoes. Sam stood with his hands on his head and turned around, allowing the detectives to cuff him. Fitz was instantly dead and lay in a large pool of blood on the street. "Jesus, you sick fuck. How could you do that to your partner?" Hugh asked him.

"He wasn't my partner, just some lily livered freak who was out for a good time." Sam responded.

Chapter 35

They called for an ambulance to process the body. The coroner came and notified Mrs. Fitzgerald. She was devastated and began crying uncontrollably. She knew her husband was into some dark things, but he was a confused man, she said. He had a good heart, and so badly wanted to fit in with others.

They took Sam to the station and began interviewing him. They wanted a detailed record of each murder to use in court. He wasn't talking just yet.

He asked for some cigarettes and coffee before he even decided to tell them anything. The men got what he asked for. He refused an attorney and was ready to talk. Charlie and Hugh sat down with Sam, still in cuffs, and began to ask him questions.

Sam was forthcoming about everything. It was like he was proud of it all and wanted to be recognized for it. He knew he was going to be put to death, but he didn't care. He was glad to share the details of his crimes.

Sam went girl by girl and told all the grizzly details. Most of them he would pick up at the coffee shop or library. The girls were always really friendly, and sometimes even willing to go for a ride with him. They had no idea he was a killer.

Charlie wanted to know about Shirley. Hugh didn't think that was a good idea.

"Tell me the details about my wife. Why did you take her?" Charlie asked.

"Are you sure you want to know that, Charlie?" Sam asked.

"What did you do to her?"

"I knew you were the lead detective on the case and I wanted to shake you up a little. I started following your wife around town, checking out her routine. She seemed lonely, like you weren't satisfying her at all."

Charlie looked at him like he wanted to kill him.

"Anyway, I parked on your street one day and she seemed a little scared. She wasn't sure what to do, but you could tell she had a bad feeling about it. The next day, I knew you were looking for me, so I went to the house and asked for you. That's when she called you at the station. As soon as I took her, I had to decide what to do with her."

Charlie felt sick. He wanted to beat the shit out of this monster and show him how he felt about him. He couldn't do it, though, and had to get him to give all the details for trial.

"So after I took her, Fitz helped me drug her, bind and gag her. We took her up to the house in the forest, and she didn't wake up for a few hours. When she did, she was cold, tired, and confused. She never begged though, even at the end."

"Of course she didn't," Charlie thought. Shirley was way too strong to give this pervert the satisfaction.

"So, I decided you weren't mad enough about the case and needed a little motivation, so I killed her."

Charlie jumped over the table and began beating the shit out of Sam. It took three detectives to get Charlie off of him. "Charlie go take a walk," Hugh told him. "You need to cool down."

After hours of interviewing Sam, they finally took him away. He was going to pay for his crimes, Charlie would see to that. Charlie felt a sense of relief that he had been caught and the case was over. But, there was a great sense of loneliness that he had no one to share it with. Shirley would have been so proud of him. He knew she was watching down on him and forgave him for everything.

Fitzgerald's funeral was Saturday. Not many people went. Some of the partners, office staff, and friends decided to pay their respects. Bobbi and Hugh went. Even though he was a monster, he was her boss for a time, and she did remember him as he was early on in their relationship. She didn't know what happened to him. Evil had consumed him and he got out of control. It was very easy for people to cross the edge, if they didn't take a step back. Fitzgerald was so insecure and wanted to be a big shot so badly, that he chose crime if that's what got him notoriety.

It was sad, really. His wife wasn't a bad person. His children were obviously embarrassed of their father, and he would only be remembered for the wrong he did in life. At the end of the service, Bobbi and Hugh decided to take a walk down to the coffee shop.

She was starting to show a little and was feeling really good. Things between them were better than ever. They had gotten married the previous week and she had never been so happy.

They met Charlie at the coffee shop and had lunch. He was doing much better. He had started spending more time with the kids and his parents. He had slowed down a little at work, and even thought about taking a desk job. His family was his first priority now. Things were slowly getting better.

Once Hugh told Bobbi that Charlie couldn't have any more kids, and there was no possibility of anyone but him being the father, Bobbi was relieved. She began to rekindle a relationship with her mother and father and things were looking up.

Bobbi's mother had been having some health issues, and the doctors said she might not improve. The timing was ironic. Right when things were going so well for them, something like this happened. Bobbi was so thankful she had reconnected with her mother. She would never forgive herself if something happened to her and they hadn't made the effort.

Bobbi's mother died right before the trial. She had been in the hospital for weeks and it had been a slow, painful death. She had heart problems. Bobbi watched her mother suffer and gasp for air for weeks. It was extremely painful and she vowed to never have issues with family members again.

The death of her mother changed Bobbi for the better. She took family much more seriously. She realized the world didn't revolve around her. She had priorities and responsibilities that were greater than herself. She thanked God every day for the lessons He had taught her.

Chapter 36

The trial had been exhausting for everyone involved. Sam sat through the entire thing without so much as a smirk. He seemed completely bored and detached. Many witnesses were called, including Fitzgerald's wife, and the people who Sam wronged in Chinatown.

When James Carlton was called, he completely sold Sam out. He told of everything shady Sam was involved in and how he had never trusted the man. Carlton proved to be a big help in sealing Sam's fate.

After the testimony, Charlie went up to Carlton and thanked him. "I really appreciate everything you have done for us during this investigation, Carlton. I know your business is not something I want to be privy to, but I want you to know, I will look the other way. You have really shown your heart and my wife and I appreciate it."

"Thank you detective. I have a wife too, and can't imagine what you've had to go through. Good luck with everything."

6 months later:

Sam was found guilty and sentenced to death, as expected. It was now his date of execution and Charlie, Bobbi, and Hugh were attending. They drove up to San Quentin in the early morning to watch this monster be put to death.

"Charlie, are you sure you're ok with all of this?" Bobbi asked.

"Yeah. I'm actually better than I thought I would be. I'm not looking forward to watching him die, but need to see it for Shirley and in order to begin my life again."

Bobbi nodded. She was having a much harder time getting around now, with the pregnancy and was absolutely glowing. They had found out they were having a girl and were going to name her Shirley. Bobbi had even introduced Charlie to a girlfriend of hers, and they had begun dating. She was so happy for Charlie and hoped things worked out.

Things between Hugh and Bobbi had never been better. He was the best husband anyone could ask for. He was so attentive and caring toward her. He never raised his voice or got upset with her. She felt so lucky every day to have him. Things had definitely come full circle for Bobbi. She had grown up, and realized what was important in life.

Hugh was proud of Charlie. He couldn't imagine moving on like he did, and accomplishing so much for the department after his wife was killed. He had worked tirelessly to create a task force preventing crimes against women in the city. Charlie had been in charge, but had created a team to carry on after he retired.

The baby was the best thing that could be happening right now. He and Bobbi were so happy and couldn't wait for the arrival of little Shirley. Things were going very well for all of them. They deserved some happiness.

As they pulled into the parking lot of San Quentin, there were people outside chanting, "Gas him! Gas him!" The public did not care for Sam, to say the least, but this was out of control. There were hundreds of people here. He obviously upset many more people than was originally thought.

The guard directed Bobbi, Hugh, and Charlie to park in the media section. They were escorted into the prison. As Bobbi walked in, she was greeted by a dark, dank space whose mood was pure evil. Hugh asked her if she was sure this was a good idea for her and the baby.

"I'll be fine, honey." She said. Bobbi had no intention of staying away from this execution. She had to see him murdered in order to forget the traumatizing events surrounding her life the past year.

Charlie and Hugh had to check their weapons in, then the three were escorted to the viewing room.

When Charlie walked in, he thought the room was odd. This was the first execution he had been present at, even though he had been a cop for years. The room was fairly dark and very quiet, even though there were about twenty people present. There were three rows of chairs in front of a pane of glass. The glass was clear and on the other side was the chamber where Sam was to be put to death. The chamber had a long table, ironically much like the one Sam used for his victims. The chamber was fairly small and stark white.

The guard escorted the three of them to their seats. They were seated in the front row. Bobbi wasn't too sure about this anymore. She had never seen a man die and didn't know if her stomach could take it. Hugh sensed her nerves.

"Honey, if you don't want to watch, you don't have to." He said. "When they start, there won't be much sound, just close your eyes."

They waited patiently for it to start.

Chapter 37

The door opened and Sam was escorted into the chamber. He was cuffed and shackled. He had on a white prison uniform and his hair was a little disheveled. He was smiling and didn't look one bit nervous to die.

He even looked at the glass and said, "Hello there everyone. Hope you enjoy the show, especially you Detective Brower." He couldn't see anyone, but knew they were there.

Charlie couldn't believe that even seconds away from his own death, he showed no remorse and was even happy to put on a show.

The attendants took the cuffs and shackles off of Sam, and forced him onto the table. He was strapped down and still appeared very calm. The doctor came in and took his vital signs before they began.

"We are ready to begin." The doctor said.

Sam still had that evil smile on his face and looked excited.

"Any last words, sir?" The doctor asked Sam.

"Yeah, you may kill me, but you'll never forget what I did. You can all go to hell."

Charlie grimaced. Why would he expect anything else from this deranged lunatic. He had no redeeming qualities.

The doctor stepped out. The lights were so bright in the execution room, that Bobbi had a hard time staying focused.

The chamber door was closed and Sam just sat there waiting for his death. A hissing sound filled the chamber and many of the people in the viewing room looked away. The gas started seeping into the chamber quickly. Sam still didn't seem afraid. He just smiled the entire time. Finally when he began to froth at the mouth and shake uncontrollably, the gas was stopped.

The doctor came into the chamber and pronounced him dead. They recorded the time of death, and the curtains were closed. The show was over. The people in the viewing room got up and began to exit.

On the way out, one of the spectators came up to Charlie and told him she was one of the victim's mother's. She wanted to personally thank Charlie and Hugh for the work they did on the case, and for being the voice for her daughter and so many others. Charlie smiled and felt renewed.

Things started to get back to normal for Charlie and the others. Charlie was spending a lot of time working on his task force. Laws had changed and women were more protected than before. Bobbi and Hugh had the baby and they were all doing well. Even Charlie was dating and enjoying his life. Until one day.

He received a phone call from Carlton. "I think you should know, Detective Brower that there is a copycat out there. He is doing everything Sam did and you need to be aware of it."

"How do you know this, Carlton?"

"My girls are turning up dead."

"We haven't seen anything about dead girls. No one has called us."

"That's because no one besides me knows they are missing. He's disposing of the bodies in a way that cannot be traced. He's chopping them up."

Charlie couldn't believe what he was hearing. A copycat killer? Why would someone want to copy anything Sam did? What the hell was wrong with people?

"Ok, buddy, I will check it out. Give me the names of your girls that have gone missing and I will look into it."

"Thanks Detective. I just don't want to see something happen like what did with Sam."

Charlie hung up the phone and called Hugh. He had taken some leave to stay home and help Bobbi with the baby. "What's up buddy?"

"We have a situation here, Hugh and I need your help."

"Sure, I'll be right down."

Hugh arrived at the station an hour later and apologized for it taking him so long.

"The baby slows us down a bit."

"Not to worry, Hugh. I got a phone call this morning from our friend James Carlton. He told me some of his girls are disappearing and he has been hearing rumors of a copycat killer, emulating Sam."

"Oh, Jesus. Just what we need. Is he sure the girls didn't just run off with someone?"

"No, he says the other girls saw one of their friends get into a car with a strange looking man, and never saw her again."

They have this code down there, that they will keep in contact with one another to stay safe. No one has seen or heard from these three girls since Monday. It was Friday. That wasn't a good sign.

"Ok, what do you want to do?" Hugh asked him.

"Let's head down to Carlton's house to get some more information." He responded.

They drove back to Carlton's and pulled up to the speaker. This looked familiar. "Detectives Brower and Fenton here to see Mr. Carlton."

"Of course," the attendant responded. "Please pull up the driveway."

They got out of the car and were greeted by Carlton in his smoking jacket. He looked tired, like he hadn't slept in days. "Geez, Carlton are you ok?" Hugh asked him.

"Not really. These girls are like my family and I can't sleep when I can't find them."

"The last time they were seen was Monday night. All three of them had gone out at different times. All three disappeared that night and haven't been heard from since."

"Well how do you know they didn't just run off?" Hugh asked him.

"They wouldn't do that. I treat them very well. They have a place to live, get paid fairly, and don't get smacked around." Carlton told him.

"Ok, Carlton, give us their names and we'll look into it." Charlie told him.

The next day, Charlie and Hugh began asking around about the girls. Most of the other prostitutes didn't believe they would just run off. "Carlton treats us good." One of the girls said.

The last time anyone had seen them had been Monday night, so the detectives wanted to go back to the area and see if anyone remembered anything. On their way over, they decided they would question people together so they could get a better feel for someone lying.

They pulled into the parking lot on the side of Grauman's. It looked like there were a lot of people out. Hugh and Charlie began talking to people on the street. No one really saw anything. They went into a few restaurants and diners and asked some of the workers. Still nothing. On the way out of one of the diner's, Hugh saw a little boy doing a magic show for tips. He went up to the child and introduced himself.

"I'm Detective Fenton, son. What's your name?"

"Jacob." The boy answered.

"Jacob, we're investigating some missing girls who were last seen around here last Monday night." Hugh told him.

"Yeah, I heard about that."

"You did? Well did you know those girls?

"Yeah, they were always really nice to me. They would watch my tricks in between customers. They even tipped me sometimes or brought me a hamburger at the end of the night."

"Oh good. They seem like they took care of you, Jacob. We need your help to take care of them, because we think they are in some trouble."

"What do you need?"

"Did you see who the girls left with that night?"

"Yes."

"Can you tell me about him?"

"Yes. His name is Dave. No one around here likes him. He's a complete jerk, always bossing everyone around."

"What do you mean bossing everyone around?"

"Well he tries to come down here and find a new girl each night. He looks like he has no money, but the girl's say he does. He acts like Mr. Big Stuff and orders the girls around, telling them to hurry up and stuff."

"And the girls listen to him?" Hugh asked.

"Well not really, but they pretend to because he pays them well."

"Do you know where Dave lives, Jacob?"

"No. No one has ever been to his house. He even takes the girls to local hotels."

"Alright, anything else you can think of to help us out?"

"Just that I saw Jackie get into the car with him about 11 p.m. and that was the last I heard from him that night."

"Thanks son. You've been a big help. Here's my card if you think of anything else ok?"

Hugh walked back over to Charlie and told him what the boy said. "He seemed to know a lot about what happens down here. Hugh told him. He says the guy comes down here every night and is named Dave. I think we should come back around 11 or so. What do you think?"

"Sounds good. We will be able to get a better feel for the scene then anyway," Charlie said.

Chapter 38

They came back around 11 that night and walked around a bit. They were dressed more casually to fit in better and avoid scaring anyone who might want to talk. The girls began walking the streets doing their normal routine. Many men approached them, but few actually offered the girls any money.

Hugh went up to some of the girls who were waiting around. "Good evening, ladies. My name is Detective Fenton, and this is my partner, Detective Brower."

"We don't talk to cops," one of the girls said and they started to walk away.

"Wait a minute. You don't understand. We were called by your boss, Carlton to find Jackie, Marie, and Betty." Charlie told them.

They stopped and turned around. "Really? Carlton is doing something about them being missing?"

"It appears so. He called us very concerned when some of you girls told him they were missing. We're out here trying to find them." Hugh said.

"They're dead. There's no point in trying to find them alive," the same girl replied.

"What do you mean? Do you know something?" Charlie asked.

"No, just a feeling."

"What do you ladies know about this man named Dave?" Hugh asked them.

"Not much, except he's a creep. He tries to order us around like we're his slaves." One of the other girls responded.

"He has some money, but makes you do awful things to earn it." The other girl added.

"So is he the type of creep that might want to hurt your friends?" Hugh asked them.

"Of course. All these men want to hurt us or they wouldn't be visiting us. He would go over the edge though to cross the line."

"Have any of you girls seen him tonight?" Charlie asked.

"No, not yet. But stick around. You're bound to run into him."

The girls walked away and Charlie and Hugh started talking.

"This guy sounds like a perfect suspect to me," Charlie said.

"We'll just have to hang around until we catch a glimpse of him."

Dave decided to head into Hollywood like he did every night about this time. He lived in Pasadena, so it was a little bit of a drive for him, but he didn't mind. Each night he left his wife and kids behind, telling them he had to go feed the homeless in L.A. They actually bought that crap! Not only did they buy it, but they were proud of him for it. You'd think his wife would wise up at some point, but whether she didn't know, or didn't want to know, he didn't care.

On the way there, he decided he was going to look for a redhead tonight. They were wild in bed and he needed to blow off some steam. His boss at the paper factory had been giving Dave a hard time lately about his lack of sales. What was he supposed to do? No one wanted any god-damned paper. Jesus. He needed a new job. Maybe he needed no job. He could just leave his family and job and jump into the car with some hot redhead. They could travel the country never slowing down.

What a nice fantasy. Why did life have to get so boring? This is why he started visiting the girl in Hollywood. They provided him with an excitement he hadn't known in years. He wished someone would've told him that getting married and having kids would kill his lifestyle. He hated having to answer to someone else. He hated having to ask permission to have a beer. It was like living with his mother all over again.

And that bitch of a mother! Dave had hated his mother for as long as he could remember. She had brought home plenty of men to keep her company after his father left them. He remembered coming home and seeing some man lying on his couch after a "session" with his mother. That's what she called them, her "sessions."

She had embarrassed both herself and Dave so much that their name was no longer good in town. She was known as nothing more than a whore and basically asked to leave. They had picked up and moved on to the next town, then the next one after that, and so on went the cycle until Dave was eighteen and could be out on his own.

His mother began to drink fairly soon after they moved for the umpteenth time. She was a mean drunk. She would scream and yell at Dave and put her cigarettes out on him for fun. His only job in life was to go get her cigarettes and bring men back to the house. He actually had to go find them for her and bring them home. It was an interesting little operation and Dave hated her every minute for it.

One day, he came home and found his mother dead lying in a pool of blood on the bed. The man who killed her was standing over her with a large butcher knife. He looked completely shocked at what he had just done. Dave was stunned, but was actually relieved that his mother was dead. The man tried to come after Dave, for fear he would tell the police what he had seen. But, Dave told the man he had hated his mother, she was a whore, and meant nothing to him. He was glad she was dead. The man took Dave in and they left town right away. No one ever solved the murder and the town thought the murderer kidnapped the boy as well.

The two traveled the country looking for a good time. The man's name was Winston, but they called him W.T. for short. W.T. and Dave were like two kids in a candy store. They traveled around helping each other commit horrible crimes. W.T. taught Dave about women and Dave helped lure them to W.T. By this time, Dave was 13 and was enjoying the attention from women. He began to develop an unhealthy obsession with them because of it.

W.T. and Dave continued to travel the country and ended up in Santa Monica, California. They loved it there. There were tons of women and it never got very cold. It was like paradise. Dave had already dropped out of school and got a job to make a living. He was working as a record shop clerk. He met so many cute teenage girls there and took them home to W.T. Once the girl's left with the good looking Dave and got to his place, they were scared to death to see another man waiting there. The two men had their way with the girls and then let them go after. They weren't killing anyone at this time.

Dave met a beautiful girl at the record store and began to date her. He thought differently of her. He didn't want to share her with W.T., so he kept her secret. He took her out on dates, kissed her softly, and began to fall in love. He hid the other part of him from her completely, and thought maybe he had changed. W.T. didn't like the fact that Dave wasn't bringing home any women any more, so he began to get frustrated and beat the boy.

Dave felt pushed into a corner by W.T. and started to feel a sense of pain like his mother has given him. He was doing the same things to Dave. Putting his cigarettes out on him, trying to beat him, all because he couldn't get his own women. Dave had had enough.

One night, Dave came home from a date with his new girlfriend and W.T. was drunk and waiting for him. He had a knife in his hand. "You know," he said, "I will kill you just like I killed your whore of a mother."

The two had a scuffle and Dave ended up stabbing W.T., killing him. Dave cleaned everything up and fled the scene. He found an apartment to rent, and began seeing his girlfriend, Cindy a few times a week. He thought the lifestyle and the killing were behind him.

Cindy and Dave continued to date. They fell in love and got married. They had children together. Dave kept this other side of him buried. Things were good for a while, then one day, Dave had had enough of Cindy's complaining and left for a while. He drove down to his old stomping grounds and found the girls. He missed the meaningless sex and power over them. He didn't have that with Cindy. She tried to control him and it made him feel like a failure as a man.

He began visiting the area every night and told Cindy that he felt like he needed to give back to the community. She bought it.

The first girl he picked up was a beautiful blonde named Jasmine. She let him take her to the hotel and do things to her that Cindy wouldn't. He was so turned on that he only lasted a few minutes. But, instead of making fun of him like Cindy would, the woman simply said, "It's ok baby. You were so excited, you couldn't help it. Wait a bit and we'll try again." He felt so comfortable with her, he was able to perform again and again.

That night he drove home with a smile on his face. It was the first time he had smiled in months, and it awoke the evil in him. He wanted to have a good time, he wanted to give into his desires.

The next night, Dave drove back to Hollywood and found a brunette. Her name was Betty, and she dressed like Bettie Page in garters and had very red lips. He picked her up and took her to the same hotel as before. The woman once again let him do many things to her that he hadn't done before. He felt a sense of control and started to boss her around. She pretended she liked it, but he didn't know she thought he was pathetic.

After he was done with her, he went home and had sex with his wife. She thought he was the most wonderful man in the world to do charity work every night.

Dave continued to visit the girls every night and things were fine, until one night. Dave picked up a woman who wasn't overly pretty but had large breasts. Dave liked that. "Get in sweetie," he told the woman.

She got into the car, and they visited the hotel once again. She had a little bit of an attitude with Dave. It had been a long night and she just wanted to go home. What she really needed was something to eat and a hot shower. "Honey, how about we make it quick and you give me $10 and I can go get something to eat?" She asked him.

This offended Dave. He wanted to take her to the hotel, romance her, be the one in charge. She was trying to control the situation and he didn't like that. "Well baby, I was hoping we could be a little more romantic than that." He told her.

She snickered a little. "You want romance honey, you probably shouldn't visit hookers."

This infuriated Dave. She was making fun of him, just like his mother had. He flew into a rage and pulled the car over. The woman thought he was just going to let her out, but she was wrong. Dave began beating her uncontrollably until the woman lie there completely limp.

Once he was done, Dave looked over at the woman's bloody body and wept. Oh, God, he thought. I've done it again. It had been years since Dave had even remembered his past and now he was falling right back into the same old habits. He was pathetic and such a complete failure. How was he going to cover this up?

Dave took the woman out to a chicken farm he knew was located outside of L.A. and pushed her naked body into the machines. Her body became little pieces, which he spread across the farm. Then he threw up, drove home, and made love to his wife.

This had happened time and time again. Dave had probably killed somewhere around 50 women. Then one day, he realized he wanted some recognition for his crimes and started leaving little clues based on the Hollywood murders he had read about last year. He wanted them to think they had a copycat killer.

Chapter 39

Dave headed into Hollywood and got out at Hollywood and Vine. He started talking to some of the girls like he always did, when one of them told Dave the cops were asking about him. "Why would they ask about me darling?" He asked her.

"Don't know Dave, but they've been asking all the girls what we know about you. You might want to get out of here tonight."

Dave was infuriated. No one was going to take away his fun for the night. He needed his fix. These damn cops thought they knew something, but they obviously didn't realize who they were dealing with. Not this time, coppers. Dave decided to ignore the warning and picked up a girl anyway. He wasn't seen by anyone and headed off to his normal hotel.

The woman was a short, petite, raven haired beauty about twenty years old. She was only too eager to go with Dave because she didn't know who he was. None of the other girls had told her, which meant she was probably new.

Dave got her into the car and headed for the hotel. They started playing a game, and Dave told her to turn around so he could blindfold her. She did as she was told. Kinky stuff usually got more money and this guy had a lot of it, you could tell.

"Ok, sweetheart, I'm going to get on top of you and tease you a little."

Dave sat on the girl and started to put his hands around her neck. She tried to act interested, but appeared a little frightened too. "Oh baby, why don't we do it, I want you now," She told him.

"Oh we're going to, darling. I'm just warming up."

He continued to put his hands around her neck and the girl realized she might be in some trouble. She began to panic and shake. Dave strangled her and left her there for the maid to find. Poor girl, he thought. She had no idea what she was getting involved in.

This time, instead of going home, Dave went to pick up another girl and took her out to the farm instead of the hotel. The girl, Charlotte, thought it was a little strange to do it on a chicken ranch, but she had seen many strange things in her seven years as a hooker. Whatever turned them on and got her the money.

"Ok, baby, what do you want me to do?" She asked him.

"Just stand there and let me look at you." He responded.

"Freak," she thought. "I have to get out of this and go home."

He had her take off her clothes and get into the pens with the chickens. "Baby, this is a little weird," She told him. Dave didn't like to be questioned. He took out his knife, ran over to her, and stabbed her over 100 times. Then he put her into the machine. Dave returned home and made love to his wife.

Charlie and Hugh couldn't find out anything about this Dave character. The girls thought he was a joke and didn't think he could be responsible for the deaths of their friends. He was a mess. He liked to be in control but that was it. None of them had ever been harmed.

Hugh felt like they were missing something. He went through the record and did a search for anyone named Dave with a record between the years of 1950 and now. Several came up. Hugh was going to spend all night going through them.

The next morning when Charlie came in, Hugh was still there. "Does Bobbi know you didn't go home last night?" Charlie asked him.

"Yeah, she told me to stay. I love that woman. Look what I found. I narrowed it down to a few Dave's in the area and I want to go check them out. Let's go to this one in Pasadena first."

They drove out to a wealthy suburb of Pasadena and began looking for the address. "Nice houses, huh?" Charlie asked him.

"It's always the nice guys who are the freaks." Hugh responded.

They pulled up to the house and got out. They put on their jackets and walked up to the front door. Hugh rang the bell and a little girl answered. "Hi, sweetie, is your mommy or daddy home?" Hugh asked her. "Just a second."

A woman came to the door and introduced herself as Cindy Jenkins. "What can I do for you gentlemen?" She asked.

"We're detectives Fenton and Brower, Ma'am and we need to ask you some questions about your husband, David Jenkins."

"Of course, come on in. Have a seat. What's this all about?"

"We're investigating a string of murders in the Hollywood areas of local call girls. We've been told his name is Dave. Your husband came up on our radar because of his previous record."

"What record?" She asked.

"He was suspected of having something to do with his mother's murder about 15 years ago. He never told you?"

"I think you obviously have the wrong person. My husband is a kind, gentle man, who would never hurt a fly. I'll have to ask you to leave now."

They got up and walked to the door. "If you think of anything suspicious or out of character for your husband, will you please give us a call? Here's my card. The murders are taking place around 11 p.m. so if he does anything out of the ordinary at that time, please let us know." Hugh told her.

Cindy closed the door and panic set it. "Oh my God," she thought. "They couldn't be talking about my husband, could they?" She started to feel sick and ran to the bathroom.

Dave had always been a little secretive about his past with her. He didn't share much with her, and she had assumed he had a tough childhood. She didn't want to press it, though. Why make him relive something painful.

He had tried to do some crazy things with her in the bedroom, which she told him flatly no. He seemed to get his feelings hurt but never brought it up again. And now, he was leaving every night for this charity work. Could these murders be tied to her husband? She needed time to think and then she would call Dave at the office.

"Dave, there were some detectives here asking about you today." She told him.

"What honey? I didn't hear you."

"Detectives. They were here today to ask questions about you."

Dave felt a little wave of panic. "What type of questions?"

"Questions about you being involved in some type of murder."

"Baby, that's nuts. They have the wrong guy."

"That's what I said, but they seemed to insist that they needed to talk to you right away."

"Ok, I will call them tomorrow to straighten this all out immediately. I'll be home in just a bit ok, darling?"

She hung up the phone and began to doubt him. "It's got to be a mistake," she thought.

Dave was distracted at work for the rest of the day. How did they find him? Those bitch hookers probably told them something that led them right to him. How was he going to fix this? He had to talk to them, but needed to come up with a story first.

Charlie and Hugh left the Jenkins house and got into the car. They both knew that Cindy was hiding something. Maybe she didn't know about the crimes, but she was starting to doubt her husband, they could see that in her face.

"What do you think? Should we go talk to her again, or let her stew on it?" Hugh asked Charlie.

"I think we should give her some time to get her husband to panic." Charlie responded.

Dave went out again that night, but was much more careful than normal. He knew Cindy was acting strange toward him, and might be doubting him. He didn't want to come home too late. If she thought he was guilty of something she would turn him in to the police in a heartbeat.

He cruised the area looking for a pretty girl. He had so much on his mind that he found it hard to focus on them. He pulled the car over and a woman came up to him.

"Hey sweetie, looking for a date?" She asked Dave.

"Maybe." Dave responded.

"How much?"

"For you, darling—twenty."

"Sounds good, hop in."

They went around the corner to a local dive bar. "Are we going to do it in the bar, sweetie?" She asked him.

Dave didn't care for her tone or her mocking him. "Maybe, is that ok with you?"

"Not exactly sweetheart. I don't give a show to anyone but you."

"Just joking, baby. How is the parking lot? I'm kind of in a hurry."

"That's fine. Let's go for it."

They started to fool around a little and things very quickly got out of hand. Dave beat the poor girl to death, then dumped her body outside of the car. He was getting sloppy by leaving her there, but he didn't care. He needed to get home to his wife. Keep his routine.

He left the parking lot quickly and made sure no one saw him. He drove home and made love to his wife. Cindy didn't act like anything was wrong, so he thought he was fine.

The next day, the detectives showed up at his work. "Dave Jenkins, we're detectives Brower and Fenton." We need to ask you a few questions about some murders we're investigating." Charlie told him.

"Sure, come on into my office." Dave responded.

"My wife said you came by yesterday. I'm so sorry to waste your time detectives, but I think you have the wrong person. My mother is alive and well in Florida. I've been doing some charity work with the homeless. I believe that might be why my name came up?"

"Not exactly. Anyway, we had another dead body found last night. Your wife tells us that you left around 7:30 last night and returned about midnight. Is that correct?" Charlie asked him.

"That sounds about right. I go help feed the homeless in Hollywood."

"For what organization?" Hugh asked him.

"I'm sorry?"

"For what organization?" Hugh repeated.

"Oh, Angels of Mercy."

"We checked with the organizations down there and they have no record of you volunteering." Charlie told him.

"I usually don't fill out information cards. I'm not there to be recognized. I just want to help."

"Oh, I see. I real generous, good-hearted guy." Charlie mocked him.

"Look, detectives, I hate to cut this short, but I have work to do, so unless you have any other questions…"

"Not for now, slick. But you can bet we'll be watching you, so be prepared." Charlie told him.

Chapter 40

Charlie and Hugh left the office and knew Dave Jenkins was their guy. "This piece of shit seriously has the nerve to tell us he's doing charity work? Wow. That's rich." Hugh said.

"We need to trail him tonight. Find out what he's doing and where he goes." Charlie said.

That night, the men followed Dave home to Pasadena and sat just down the street from his house. They waited for him to leave again, but he didn't. He never left the house. It was like he knew they were watching him and weren't going to take that chance.

"Son of a bitch won't leave tonight. We'll have to come back tomorrow." Charlie said.

They drove off and went home. Charlie went home to spend some time with his kids. Hugh went home to spend some time with Bobbi and the baby.

Dave got up the next morning and felt pretty proud of himself that he outsmarted the detectives. They thought they could follow him home and stake him out without him knowing? He was much smarter than that. He would just go out after work tonight. He would tell Cindy he had a meeting then would go to Hollywood after that. She would be fine with it.

After work, Dave headed out for a quick bite. He had a few drinks and was ready to cruise around looking for girls. He drove up to some of his favorites on Hollywood Blvd. "Hey Dave, how are you honey?" One of the girls asked.

"I'm doing good baby. You want some company tonight?"

"You know it. Where do you want to go?"

"How about get in and we'll figure it out."

She got in and he took her up to Griffith Park. He wanted to impress her, to prove that he wasn't just some john. That he had skills to romance these girls. She fell for it.

"Oh Dave, baby this place is gorgeous. What have I done to deserve this?" She asked.

"Oh, nothing's too good for you sweetheart. Now, how about take off your clothes and let's have some fun?"

She started to get undressed and Dave looked upset.

"What's the matter sweetheart?" She asked.

"You're not a true redhead." Dave told her.

"So? What does that matter?"

"Get out of the car."

He made her get out in the cold and told her to walk back. She was so angry she screamed and yelled at him, not knowing how lucky she was to be spared.

When she got back to town after taking a cab, she told all the girls what he did to her. It would be a cold day in hell before one of them went anywhere with Dave.

The next night Dave tried to pick up a girl in the same area. No one would get in the car with him. He was downright pissed. "What the fuck's your problem Daisy?" He called after one of the girls as she walked away from him. He drove off and headed for Chinatown, where the low class hookers were.

He pulled up into Chinatown and a few of the girls came over to his car. He chose one and took off with her. There were plenty of seedy hotels in the area where no one would recognize him. He could hurt her and leave her there without anyone knowing.

When they got to the hotel room, the girl began to undress. He told her how beautiful she was and then they began to make love. Dave got comfortable and decided to go for her throat. She wrapped his hands around her neck and she looked a little uncomfortable. She went along with it though and they tried again.

This time, Dave was a little too forceful. He scared the girl and she began to panic telling him to get off of her. He became angry and squeezed tighter until she was ready to pass out. Somehow she got him off of her and ran screaming out into the hall. She ran down to the desk clerk and told him to call the police. Dave didn't know what to do, so he snuck out one of the emergency exits. This was a costly mistake and if the girl identified him, he was through.

The girl was standing in her underwear crying hysterically waiting for the police to arrive. Dispatch had called for Hugh and Charlie and they were on their way. The desk manager got the girl a robe and offered her something to eat while she waited. He felt sorry for her.

Hugh and Charlie walked into the hotel and asked for the manager. He came out and escorted the detectives to his office. "This is the young lady we called you about," he said. "She has been crying since she came down here." The desk clerk told them.

They walked into the office and approached the woman. "Sweetheart, we're detectives Fenton and Brower. Can you tell us what happened to you?" Hugh asked her.

She was so shaken up, she could barely talk. "A man brought me here and tried to kill me." She told them. "He was trying to choke me, I got free and ran down here."

Charlie knew this sounded like something Dave Jenkins was capable of. "Do you remember what he looked like?" He asked her.

She nodded. "If we show you some pictures, can you point him out to us?"

She nodded again.

This was the break they needed. If she could identify Dave Jenkins from some photos, he would be arrested, case closed.

They took the woman down to the station and gave her some coffee and got her something to eat. She called her sister to come down and comfort her. While they waited for some photos to come up, Hugh called to check on Bobbi.

"Everything ok, honey?" He asked her.

"Yes, babe. Shirley is doing fine. I've been having some chest pains today though. It's feeling a little like indigestion. I'm going to bed a little early, so can we talk in the morning?"

"Of course, honey. Will you please call me if you need anything? I mean it."

"I will, babe. Goodnight."

He hung up the phone and made a point of telling himself to take her for a checkup. He worried about her and loved her more than life itself.

Dave panicked. He didn't know where to go or what to do. It was surely a matter of time before the girl identified him. He couldn't go home. He wasn't ready to give up his family life yet, though. He had to think.

He pulled into a hotel and got a room. He called Cindy and told her things were really bad down here tonight and he was going to stay, so he wasn't too tired to drive. He would use the night to think and have a plan in the morning.

Morning came and Dave knew he could go home. Even with the photo, the police had no evidence that he did anything to the other girls. There was nothing for them to arrest him on other than trying to assault the girl. He would be arrested, Cindy's trust would be broken, but no jail time.

He could deal with that. He would have to tell Cindy that he made a mistake and would never do it again. But, he wouldn't be arrested for murder. He drove home and waited for the police to come. They never did.

The girl was too afraid of Dave to tell the police who he was. She refused to do a lineup after her sister arrived at the station. Her sister told her it was dangerous and they didn't need any trouble for the family. The girl agreed and told the detectives she couldn't do it. She had made a mistake.

"Great, just great." Charlie said. "That was the break we needed to arrest Jenkins. That piece of shit is still out walking around free to try to kill again. Maybe next time the girl won't be so lucky. We have to move quickly on this, Hugh."

"We will, buddy. Don't give up. Let's go put some pressure on him. We'll talk to some people at his company to make him uncomfortable. Maybe he'll get angry with us and try something." Hugh told him.

The two detectives drove over to the paper factory and asked for Jenkins' supervisor. A small, older gentleman with a kind disposition came out to the front. "What can I do for you gentlemen?" He asked.

"We're here to ask you some questions about an employee of yours, Dave Jenkins." Charlie told him.

"Dave Jenkins quit yesterday and said he had to leave the area unexpectedly," the supervisor told the men.

Charlie and Hugh just looked at one another dumbfounded.

TO BE CONTINUED...

About The Author

Kori Donahue is a high school English teacher, who has been teaching for 10 years. This is her first novel, and she is planning on continuing the series very soon. Her spare time is spent blogging (www.blondeepisodes.com), reading, writing, and spending time with family and friends. She currently lives in Los Angeles, with her yorkie, Mimi La Rue.

About Murder On The Boulevard

Bobbi had always wanted to find Mr. Right, but, as a young, independent woman in her late 20's, Hollywood was probably not the right place to find him, especially in the 1950's.

Just when she thinks she's found her Prince Charming, she gets involved in something sinister. Bodies are appearing all over town, and if she doesn't figure it out soon, she'll be the next murder victim…On The Boulevard.